CHARLIE

Gloria Repp

journey**forth**®

Greenville, South Carolina

Library of Congress Cataloging-in-Publication Data

Repp, Gloria, 1941–
  Charlie / by Gloria Repp.
    p. cm.
Book two of a three-part fictional history: "Adventures of an Arctic
missionary."
Summary: In the Alaska Territory in 1951, two young missionaries
worry about how to fight superstition, especially that of one young
boy, but a surprise gift of the gospel of Mark translated into Eskimo
brings hope.
  ISBN 1-57924-817-9 (alk. paper)
  [1. Missionaries—Fiction. 2. Eskimos—Fiction. 3. Superstition—
Fiction. 4. Christian life—Fiction. 5. Alaska—History—20th cen-
tury—Fiction.] I. Title.
  PZ7.R296 Ch 2002
  [Fic]—dc21
                                                          2002009866

Designed by Jamie Leong Miller
Cover by Dennis Dzielak
Illustrations by David Schuppert

© 2002 BJU Press
Greenville, South Carolina 29609
JourneyForth Books is a division of BJU Press.

Printed in the United States of America

ISBN 978-1-57924-817-8
eISBN 978-1-60682-871-7

15 14 13 12 11 10 9 8 7

For Andrew Enjaian,

who keeps on persevering.

Books by Gloria Repp

The Secret of the Golden Cowrie
The Stolen Years
Night Flight
A Question of Yams
Noodle Soup
Nothing Daunted
Trouble at Silver Pines Inn
Mik-Shrok
The Mystery of the Indian Carvings
Charlie

Contents

Have not I commanded thee?
Be strong and of a good courage;
be not afraid, neither be thou dismayed.

Joshua 1:9

1 Am-nok

The drums beat on and on. Their low voices filled the cabin, muttering of great deeds to come. Steve Bailey leaned against the rough walls of the *kazhim,* the community house of the village, and tried to find a more comfortable position. He had waited more than an hour in this crowd of swaying, chanting Eskimos.

It was Joseph, one of the few Eskimos Steve knew in Shanaluk, who had invited him to the kazhim. "Come see Am-nok," Joseph had said. "He talk to spirits and get good hunting. He bring caribou. You see."

Maybe Joseph just wanted to show him that the shaman could do more powerful things than a white missionary, but Steve had come anyway.

Charlie was here too. He'd seen the boy wedged into a clump of young Eskimos, standing as close as possible to the drummers. His face shone, and something about the look in his eyes worried Steve. Did Charlie really believe in this shaman? He certainly wasn't as skeptical as his father, Tignak.

Steve searched the crowd again for Tignak. No, the old Eskimo must have decided not to come.

He took a deep breath, then wished he hadn't. The air in here was stifling—thick with odors of seal oil and wood smoke and sweat and something that Liz called "that fishy smell." He gazed around the kazhim, at the walls hung with skins, at the platform where Am-nok would stand, at the smiling, expectant faces. He and Liz had been in Alaska for only a few months, but already he knew that the Eskimos hid many fears beneath those smiles.

Feet stamped in the snow outside, and Joseph twisted toward the door. "Am-nok come! You see!"

The drums grew louder, the door opened, and Am-nok entered in a cloud of frosty air. The shaman carried a mask that resembled an animal's face, and from his belt dangled animal teeth and claws and small carved figures.

He paused in the middle of the room, surveying the crowd. The drums quieted. He hoisted his large body onto the platform, and the rattles on his leggings made a dry, whispering sound.

Raising one arm, he proclaimed something in a high voice, and for the hundredth time Steve wished he knew more Eskimo. The people shouted in response.

Am-nok's eyes fastened on Steve. "This nothing for great white man look at," he said. "These people foolish come here."

Steve inclined his head politely. "I would like to listen to Am-nok's wisdom."

The shaman's lips twisted in his plump face. "Even white man born foolish." His voice hardened. "No. You go now."

Joseph took Steve's arm, and everyone leaned out of the way as he stumbled to the door. A minute later he found himself outside the kazhim, alone.

He stood there in the fading afternoon light, breathing the fresh, icy air and listening to the rising frenzy of drums inside. After a minute he turned slowly toward Tignak's cabin.

If it weren't for Ben Tignak, he wouldn't even be in Shanaluk. He and Liz had traveled here from their home village of Koyalik because the old Eskimo had taken a liking to them and asked them to come back.

This morning Steve had preached to a small group of men, and they seemed to listen when Tignak translated the English words into Eskimo. He had wanted to have another meeting this afternoon, but that wasn't going to happen now. Am-nok had stolen his audience away.

2 Mask of the White Fox

Steve paused to stamp the snow from his mukluks at the door of Tignak's storm porch, and in keeping with Eskimo custom, went into the cabin without knocking. The grandmother rose from her rocking chair to pour hot tea for everyone, and his wife met him with an anxious look.

He tried to sound cheerful. "Well, everything went okay until the shaman showed up. Drums, chanting, lots of anticipation." He hung his parka on a wooden peg and looked over at Tignak, who sat in his moose hide chair by the stove. "Am-nok decided that this white man should not be permitted to stay."

For a moment Tignak did not answer. He accepted a steaming mug from the grandmother and nodded his thanks. Then he said, "Many families in the village are hungry, and we have not seen any caribou for a long time. Perhaps Am-nok thought you would disrupt the spirits."

Steve sat down at the table with his tea and stirred sugar into it. Liz, sitting beside him, turned to Tignak. "Tell us about Am-nok," she said. "Are the people afraid of him?"

"Not afraid, exactly. They respect him. He claims to be able to speak with the spirits, and many believe that he is very powerful."

Liz glanced at Steve. "Is there a shaman in Koyalik?"

"I don't think so." He sipped at his tea, hoping he was right.

"Probably not," said Tignak. "There are not many shamans left in this part of Alaska, and Am-nok prefers to hold his meetings in secret. The white man is changing the way we Eskimos live."

Shadows crept across the log walls as the short February day ended, and Tignak got up to light a kerosene lantern. The grandmother spoke in Eskimo from where she stood at the stove. Tignak answered; then he smiled. "Soon we will eat. I know some things about Koyalik, but I have a few more questions for you."

As the moments ticked past, Steve wondered what was happening at the kazhim. When would Charlie get back? He wanted to ask Tignak about the boy's interest in Am-nok but hesitated, thinking that the old Eskimo might be offended by such a personal question.

He ate the thick, dark stew in silence, chewing thoughtfully on the gristly joints of moose meat. He listened as Liz chattered to Tignak and somehow managed to communicate cheerfully with the grandmother.

A young girl, perhaps ten years old, appeared from the back room and silently accepted a bowl of stew from the grandmother. She perched on a bunk in the corner and watched them while she ate, her soft black eyes following Liz's every move.

Darkness fell outside. The grandmother lit another lantern, and its yellow light flickered over the smoke-stained logs of one wall. She refilled their cups with hot black tea, and then, with a shy smile, served the cookies Liz had brought.

Surely the meeting would be over soon.

Tignak dropped several short lengths of peeled wood onto the table and pulled out his knife. "Tell me now, about the school in Koyalik."

Steve looked at Liz, and she answered. "The teacher is a white man, Gus Svenson, who also runs the Trading Post. I used to teach too, so I went to visit their school a couple of times. Gus has a heart for the children—they really seem to love him. I was amazed at how fast they learn."

She picked up one of the pieces of wood. "What are you going to make?"

"Fish trap." Tignak's knife flashed over the wood, cutting it into strips. "My little Sarah likes to learn from books. She is reading to me already."

Steve glanced over at the bunk, but Sarah had disappeared.

"Now, Charlie," Tignak said, "he does not care for school. He is—what do you call it in the States?—a teenager. He likes to listen to the shaman's stories and to hunt. He killed his first caribou when he was eight years old."

Steve laughed. "I never liked school very much either. Always wanted to be outside."

Tignak picked up another piece of wood. "And now you are a preacher?"

"Yes. I came to talk about what God says in His book, the Bible." An inadequate statement, but perhaps it would do for now.

"I have read in the Bible," Tignak said politely. He glanced up, his gaze as sharp as his knife. "Why did you come to the Eskimos? Why not the Africans? Or the South Americans?"

Steve took a drink of tea. What a question! He couldn't say, "God called me to the Eskimos." It would mean nothing to these people, even to this clever old man.

Liz came to his rescue. "Tell him how it began," she said. "About Sergeant Preston."

Tignak raised an eyebrow, sending wrinkles up his forehead. "Sergeant Preston?"

Steve had to laugh at the look on his face. "Sergeant Preston of the Northwest Mounted Police. When I was a kid, I used to listen to the radio serials about Preston and his dog—Yukon King. And later I read about men like Peary and Amundsen who spent their lives exploring the Arctic. I fell in love with the land, I guess. Eventually I learned about the Eskimos, and I thought they were a remarkable people."

He leaned forward. "That's why I want to tell them about God; that He loves them."

Tignak put his knife aside and stood up, more abruptly than usual. He opened the stove and poked in more wood. Over his shoulder, he asked, "And how is your study of Eskimo coming?"

"Slowly," said Steve. "You told me it's a complicated language, and you're right! I wish more people in Koyalik could speak English."

But knowing English hadn't helped Victor accept Christ, he reminded himself. Not yet.

Tignak had returned to the table, and now he jabbed at the air with his knife, his dark eyes intent. "It is most important for every Eskimo to learn English. Someday soon, Alaska will become a state, and Eskimos must learn to deal with white men and speak their language."

Liz leaned toward him, her elbows on the table. "You really think Alaska will be granted statehood?"

"Exactly," said Tignak. "Alaska has been a territory of the United States for . . . how long? Longer than you or I can remember. It is a rich country, the population is growing, and here it is 1951, and we still aren't allowed to govern ourselves. It's only a matter of time."

He picked up two of the wood strips and began to weave them together. While he and Liz talked politics, Steve wondered again about Charlie, hoping that Am-nok's ceremony wouldn't take all night. At least Tignak wasn't one of the shaman's followers.

Accidentally meeting Tignak a few months ago had turned out to be one of God's great blessings. Tignak was well educated; he'd been a scout during World War II and a guide in Fairbanks for years. He had welcomed them to Shanaluk and they'd had some good conversations. All because of a blizzard last fall.

Come to think of it, he'd better check on the weather now. He stepped to the window and scratched a hole in the frost to look out.

Vast snowfields stretched to the horizon, glittering like frozen silver. One of the dogs, probably Howler, raised his voice in complaint to the moon, and from the darkness came the quivering answer of a wolf.

He looked back at Tignak. "The moon's up. What do you think the weather's going to be like tomorrow?"

"Clear, for once. We've had plenty of storms this year. You might be wise to grab your chance of getting home."

"I'd hoped to have another meeting."

Tignak shook his head. "Not tomorrow. After the ceremony, they'll dance all night, and tomorrow their heads will be full of Am-nok's words."

Steve seized on the skeptical note in the Eskimo's voice. "Do you think he has any genuine power?"

"Am-nok has power." Tignak paused in his weaving. "I do not understand Am-nok's power, but I suspect that it is connected with the spirits, and I know the spirits are real. Sometimes it frightens me to think about that."

The weathered old face was somber. "Many shamans are just noise and trickery. They get themselves worked up and try to put on a good show for the people. Am-nok does that, and more besides."

Tignak turned up the lantern, and the circle of light widened on the scarred wooden surface of the table. Steve watched as the Eskimo slid another wood strip into place. Perhaps soon he could tell Tignak about Christ's power over the spirits.

Footsteps crunched outside and stamped through the storm porch. "Here's Charlie!" Tignak sounded relieved.

Charlie burst through the doorway, letting in a blast of icy air. His face glowed, and his eyes burned with excitement. "Am-nok—he wear mask of the white fox. He beat on drums and he talk to the spirit of the fox." Charlie shivered at the memory. "He ask for help to find caribou."

The boy gave his father a challenging stare. "The mask, it stuck to his face. He didn't hold it on."

"They grasp it with their teeth," Tignak said quietly.

"He talk to the spirits, and they help him. He bring the caribou close by so we have good hunting."

Charlie glanced at Steve. "We hear the voice of the spirit. It come from behind the stove."

Tignak nodded and went on with his weaving. "Am-nok is good at throwing his voice." He gestured at the table. "We saved cookies for you, son. Would you like some with your tea?"

"Sure." Charlie flashed a smile at Liz. "I like your cookies."

The boy crunched into a peanut butter cookie, and Steve remembered that Liz had sent cookies along on that first trip last November—the time he'd ended up in Shanaluk by mistake—and again when he'd come in December. This was his fourth trip to Shanaluk, and they'd come with high hopes of really accomplishing something. Now this! And they had to leave tomorrow.

He tried to shake off his worry about Am-nok's influence. He and Liz would come again. They would keep praying for Tignak and his family. And they would pray about this need for caribou too.

Midmorning the next day, an orange sun was just rising when Steve went out to pack the sled and harness the dogs. He found Charlie crouched in the snow with an arm around Mikki, talking to him. The sleek gray husky lifted his head and waved his plumed tail in welcome. The other dogs yipped and yowled as Steve shook out the harness and set to work.

As usual, he had to break up a fight between Bandit and Patch, but the team seemed to be in good health and eager to run. Liz soon emerged from the cabin with the duffle bag and the rest of their baggage, and Charlie helped to rope everything onto the sled.

He paused to grin at Steve. "That Mik-shrok, he one fine dog." Charlie pulled the rope taut and tied it swiftly. "That Mik-shrok must be part wolf. Very sma-a-a-rt. He know everything I say."

Steve scratched behind Mikki's floppy ear. "How can you tell?"

"He have light in his eye," Charlie said seriously. "I can tell." He gave one more tug on the rope, and the sled was packed.

Liz climbed up onto the pile of baggage, sat down, and grabbed the rope with both hands. "All set!"

Steve shook hands with Tignak one last time while the dogs pranced and jiggled impatiently, then he stepped onto the runners and spoke to Mikki. The husky lunged forward, his teammates jerked into action, and the sled leaped through the snow. Steve looked back and waved.

Charlie's solemn face broke into a grin. He lifted one arm, Eskimo fashion, and called out a farewell that sounded like *"Watzcookun!"*

Steve waved again and turned the sled across the tundra. How soon could they make another trip to Shanaluk? Tignak's remark burned in his mind: "Their heads will be full of Am-nok's words."

But the men of Shanaluk needed *God's* words. Tignak seemed interested. Charlie seemed to be listening. *Please, Lord, bring us back soon.*

3   Caribou Hunt

The dogs ran steadily toward the frozen Tiskleet River that would serve as their highway into Koyalik. Steve gazed across the snow-covered tundra. What a backyard! Thousands of square miles of wilderness—tundra, river delta, and mountains—with just a few Eskimos living here and there.

He flipped the fur ruff of his parka forward, making a warm cave that would keep out the wind. It wasn't especially cold for February: only twenty-five below, according to the thermometer outside Tignak's cabin, and Liz looked almost comfortable on her bumpy perch. He whistled softly to himself. It was a good day for traveling.

His thoughts circled round to Charlie, and to the boy's peculiar farewell. The word he had used didn't sound much like Eskimo.

When they stopped to rest the dogs, he lit a small fire, using twigs from the nearby willows that poked through the snow. Liz brought an armful of dead willow branches, and soon they'd melted enough snow to water the dogs and make tea. While he stirred sugar into his tea, he asked Liz if she'd heard what Charlie said when they left.

"I sure did!" She smiled, cradling her steaming mug in both hands. "You know what? I think he's been listening to some of Tignak's American friends. Sounds to me like he's picked up some slang."

Steve frowned. *"Watz . . ."*

"Remember how the kids always used to say, *What's cookin', good lookin'?*"

"That's it! *What's cookin'!*" He laughed. "What a kid!"

Mikki butted against his knee, and Steve looked down at the husky's intelligent white-masked face. "Charlie sure likes you, Mik. He's one sma-a-art boy, isn't he? Ready to take us home? Okay, let's go!"

"I'm going to walk beside the sled for a while," said Liz. "You know what, Steve? I think we should pray about this Am-nok and his claim that he's going to find caribou. I hope God will send some meat, but I want Him to get the glory."

"I do too."

After Liz had walked for an hour, she took a turn standing on the runners behind the sled, and Steve trotted beside her, watching the dogs with pleasure. They ran easily in long, loping strides, ears pointed forward. They worked well together: thin, nervous Howler; solid, brown Bigfoot; Bandit and one-eyed Patch, both rascals; and Mikki, the leader. From somewhere came the *qwawk* of a raven, and the whole team speeded up.

Steve squinted at the sun, still overhead. "At this rate, we'll get to Koyalik before dark. I want to go up to the Trading Post, first thing. Koyalik has hungry people too, and some of the men were supposed to go hunting."

Liz looked down the river, as if she could already see the huddle of Eskimo cabins that was Koyalik. "I wonder how Victor and Nida are doing." She laughed. "We've only been gone a few days! You'd think it was weeks."

By the time Steve got to the Trading Post, its general store was crowded with Eskimos who were shopping or visiting. He spoke to several men and waved to others. Gus, the old trader, wasn't in his usual place behind the counter. Must be in the back.

Steve walked through the small room that served as office and post office, and poked his head into the kitchen.

"Steve!" A tall, bearded man had been tasting something from a battered pot on the stove. He put down his spoon and stepped into the post office. "Mail plane finally made it in today. Looks like Liz's mother hasn't forgotten you two." He handed a letter to Steve and went back to the stove. "Excuse me. Can't let my stew burn. Where've you been?"

"Thanks, Gus." Steve leaned against the table. "It was quite a trip."

When he described what Am-nok had done, the trader stopped stirring long enough to rub at the bald spot on his head. "Yah?"

"I've been wondering—is there a shaman in Koyalik?"

"No," Gus said, "but every once in a while they talk about Am-nok here. In these modern days, you'd be surprised how many Eskimos are still afraid of the spirits. Especially the bad spirits, the *tungat.*"

"Not at all surprised," said Steve, remembering the odd behavior of Victor and the others this past fall. "The people of Koyalik think we have tungat in our cabin, you know. And sure enough, they won't step inside our door."

"That's right. Too bad old Patik never got properly buried. Don't worry, one of these days they'll decide it's safe enough to pay you a visit. Oh, did you run into Victor yet? He was looking for you."

"I'll find him," said Steve. "Did the hunters get a caribou?"

"Nope. Every couple of years the caribou change their route, and people get really worried." Gus pushed his pot to one side on the big black stove and began filling a kettle with water.

"Because they don't have money to buy meat at the store?"

"It's more than that. They use caribou hides for clothes and mattresses, leg skins for mukluks, sinews for thread, antlers for tools."

"I didn't know that. It's worse than I thought." Steve fastened his parka. "I'm going to try and catch up with Victor."

Outside the trading post, a tall young Eskimo hailed him in careful English. "Steve! Good to see you back. I hunt tomorrow. Want to come?"

"Sure do, Vic." Steve paused in the gathering darkness. "I heard that the hunters didn't get anything."

"No caribou. Not yet." Victor seemed deep in thought as they walked together down the wide, snow-packed lane that ran through the center of Koyalik. But he said nothing more until he turned onto a small path leading to his cabin. "I see you tomorrow. Early. Bring dogs, okay?"

Steve hurried home to finish unpacking the sled and repack it for tomorrow. He would travel light so there'd be plenty of room in the sled for meat, but he'd better take both rifles, his hunting knife, some bannock, and the axe, of course. He was sharpening the axe when Liz came in.

"I went to see Nida." She stamped the snow off her mukluks and stood them inside the door. "I sure hope you get something. From what Nida said, there's no meat left in the whole village. I told her I'm praying that God will send a huge herd of caribou, just for Koyalik."

She held out a pair of boots that were made of caribou skin and trimmed with dark fur. "Nida made you some new mukluks. She even put some of that grass inside too."

"That's really nice of her." Steve glanced down at his feet. "But I was going to wear my old hunting boots this trip. They seem to work better with snowshoes."

"That's because they're what you're used to," Liz said. "Well, I'll put them in your duffle bag, just in case."

He grinned at her. "You're good at that, you know."

"What?"

"That 'just in case' stuff. Don't worry about me; this is just a little hunting trip. And I know you'll be praying."

Long before sunrise the next morning, Steve and his dogs joined Victor at the edge of the frozen lagoon. The young Eskimo's eyes sparkled as brightly as the stars overhead. "I go to check my traps—yesterday—and I see wolf sign. I think maybe caribou around there." He gave Steve a sideways glance. "My brother, the one who live up the river, he go to Shanaluk. The shaman there say he bring caribou soon. May be today."

Am-nok again.

Steve chose his words carefully. "We've been praying that the Lord would send caribou. I hope He does."

Victor made no reply. He swung into place behind his sled and pointed up the river, into the starlit darkness.

More than an hour later, they reached Victor's first string of traps, set close to the river bank. The traps were empty, but tracks—small five-toed tracks—circled past them.

Steve bent over the tracks. Wolverine. Too smart to step into even an Eskimo's trap.

CHARLIE

Victor snorted in disgust at the sight of the wolverine tracks and went to examine the snow drifts at the edge of the river. "Wolf here!" He pointed at two sets of four-toed tracks leading off into the tundra. "Now we go this way."

The dogs labored to pull the sleds up through the drifted snow on the river bank, but when they reached the tundra, Victor's lead dog lifted his muzzle, his head turning this way and that. One of the huskies yelped, and Steve's dogs took off at a run so suddenly that he had to jump onto the runners or get left behind. They must have caught the scent of some animal.

Caribou?

Another hour passed, but the dogs seemed tireless. They dashed across the snow, bouncing the sleds over rough spots, as they followed the line of wolf tracks.

They reached the top of a small rise that was almost un-noticeable in the white landscape. Victor slowed the dogs to look around, as if he knew this place.

Ahead lay a cluster of snow-covered boulders and the bristles of leafless willow shrubs. The wolf tracks went down the slope toward the boulders, then seemed to vanish.

Puzzled, Steve studied the ground. Then he saw that the wolf tracks had disappeared into snow that was hard-packed by many hooves. Caribou.

Victor gave a grunt of satisfaction, and they took the dogs down to the bottom of the hill, where they tethered the teams behind the rocks.

Victor unlashed his gun from the sled. "Now we wait."

It seemed a long wait to Steve, while the pink light of dawn crept toward them from the horizon, tinting the broad tundra, the snow-capped boulders, and the broken snow of the caribou's trail. Cold seeped through his heavy parka and the layers of wool beneath. He and Victor stood quietly or walked about swinging their arms to keep warm.

Following Mikki's example, the dogs had curled up in the snow, but from time to time, one of them would lift his nose to the wind and whine.

Suddenly Victor's lead dog sprang to his feet, trembling with excitement. Victor muttered something to him in Eskimo and he sank back down, but every dog was looking to the north.

"Coming," said Victor.

Steve looked to the north, but he couldn't see anything. From the distance came a low rumble, like the sound of a heavy, slow train. A few black dots appeared, then more and more. Looked like a good-sized herd. If only he could get one!

Suddenly the plain was filled with lean, cinnamon-brown bodies surging across the snow. They ran so close that he could hear their grunting breaths. The bulls were magnificent in their winter coloring, with glistening white manes and great upward-sweeping antlers.

Victor stepped out from behind the rocks, almost into the path of the thundering caribou, and raised his rifle. Steve edged far enough out to get into good position, but he kept a careful distance from the herd.

One shot from Victor, and a buck dropped. Then another shot and another kill. Victor shot again and again. The stream of caribou parted and flowed around the fallen bodies as if nothing had happened.

The dogs leaped to their feet, barking wildly, straining at their harness.

Steve took aim at a galloping buck. The gun slammed into his shoulder, a crack rang out, and the snow puffed. Too high.

He chambered another shell and aimed lower this time. *Whump.* The buck staggered away from the herd and went down.

He shouted in triumph, turning to follow it, but Victor's arm knocked him sideways into the snow. A wild-eyed bull, its white mane flying, charged over the place where he'd stood.

Slowly Steve got to his feet, brushing snow off his parka. His shoulder hurt as if it had been hit by a baseball bat, but at least he hadn't been flattened by caribou hooves.

"Good thing you saw him, Vic," he said. "What got into that one?"

"Wolf make them crazy. Sometimes run in circles. Always watch." Victor stared after the last of the herd, which was disappearing rapidly into the distance. Off to one side, two gray shapes loped after the stragglers.

Victor cuffed his dogs into quiet, and they settled down again, watching his every move. Howler sat stiffly, his mouth open and pink tongue dripping, his ears quivering with anticipation.

The young Eskimo grinned broadly. "So far so good. Now we have meat." He took out his knife and bent over one of the bucks he had killed. He started with a quick cut down the animal's chest. "Nice and fat!"

Steve hurried over to look at his own buck. It wasn't as big as Victor's, and not as fat, but it would provide meat for the village. "Thank you, Lord!" he exclaimed.

Victor gave him a sideways glance, and Steve didn't care. God had been merciful to answer prayer. Why should Am-nok get the credit?

The dogs whimpered eagerly at the scent of blood, but Victor ignored them and set to work, barehanded in the cold. A raven circled overhead, waiting its turn.

Steve helped him to skin the caribou and cut the meat into quarters. "I've never seen a herd run like that in my whole life," he said. "I wish Liz could have been here."

Victor flicked his knife through the meat, cutting out the deer's tongue with extra care. "For Nida," he said happily. "She like. You take yours for Liz?"

Steve tried to imagine how Liz would react if he brought her the tongue of a caribou as a gift. She'd be okay, but . . .

He wiped his blood-stained knife in the snow. "Give it to Nida as a present from me. Tell her you saved my life today. I'll take the antlers for Liz; she'll want to hang them up somewhere."

Victor smiled and shrugged, probably marveling at the strangeness of white men.

CHARLIE

They loaded some of the meat onto Victor's sled but left most of it in the snow, securely covered with hides to keep off the wolves and wolverines. It would be picked up later.

How could anyone be sure of finding this spot again? When Steve asked, Victor looked vague. "I know. The others, they know this place too."

While the dogs ate their share of the kill, Steve packed his meat and hide onto the sled and tied the pair of antlers on top. He ran a finger down the front tines, which swept forward in graceful curves. The back tines rose above them in elegant points of bone, dark as polished brown wood. He couldn't wait to see the look on Liz's face.

They turned the heavily laden sleds back toward the river. It was slow going now, and the dogs were tired, but pale sunlight still shone down upon them, glinting on the rich brown of the antlers.

After less than an hour, Victor halted his team and waited until Steve drew alongside. "I go check my other traps." He gestured off across the tundra. "River right ahead. You know the way. Take meat to the Trading Post."

"Sure," said Steve. "And I'll tell them you're coming."

Victor swung his sled to the north and lifted an arm in farewell.

"*Gih,* Mikki!" Steve called. "Let's get going. They're all waiting for us." Mikki jumped ahead, stretching the towline tight, and they set off in an arc of powdered snow.

Steve was watching for the line of willows that marked the river's edge when snow began to fall. The flakes were large and light, drifting lazily. They piled in glittering ridges along the dark sweep of the antlers and made a lacy white covering for the rapidly freezing caribou meat, the guns, and the axe.

Minutes later, the snow changed, becoming as fine and dry as salt. The dogs kept running, but their feet and the runners of the sled threw back a snow cloud that was filled with crystalline needles of ice.

Steve hunched deeper into his parka and peered ahead. How far to the river?

From the swirling white horizon came wind, and with it a white mist that blotted out the entire tundra. The dogs slowed, but they did not stop. Good. He let them go, hoping they would stay on track for the river.

He brushed a mittened hand back and forth in front of his face like a windshield wiper. Couldn't see anything in this stuff. Seemed to be losing his sense of direction. He lifted his snowshoes carefully in the deepening snow and kept one hand on the handlebars.

The sled plunged through a snowdrift, almost tipping over, and narrowly missed a thicket of willows. The Tiskaleet River, at last.

He turned the team onto the river ice, and, after a moment's hesitation, Mikki obeyed. The dogs must be getting tired. He'd keep off the sled for a while so they wouldn't have to pull his weight. "Good dogs," he yelled into the white nothingness. "*Gih,* Mikki, *gih,* Howler!"

4 Whiteout

After another hour of traveling through endless white, Steve stopped the team for a rest. The dogs dropped to the snow, panting, and began to lick the ice out of their paws. At least they weren't hungry, not after eating all that caribou.

He hurried to melt some snow—lukewarm for them, scalding hot for himself. There was nothing to look at but snow, and the longer he stared into it, the more it seemed to swirl. As soon as the dogs finished drinking, he started them off again.

In spite of the hot drink, aching cold crept through the woolen gloves and fur mittens on his hands and settled into the shoulder that Victor had bruised.

How long would this last? A whiteout for sure. Gus had told him that a whiteout was caused by a layer of warm air settling above a layer of cold air, and that the peculiar effects could play tricks on a man's mind.

It was strange how the whirling snowflakes glittered, as if they were reflecting an invisible sun. He squinted ahead. Maybe it was because of the reflected light that he couldn't see two feet in front of his face. He could hear the dogs still pulling steadily, but even the familiar sounds of their panting breaths and running feet were oddly distant, disconnected.

White shadows floated around his head, then flew past. One minute they were trees, then cabins, then rocky cliffs.

Am-nok's face appeared, wearing a twisted grin, then faded away.

Mirages? Yes. Gus had told him about those too. The old trader had also advised him never to travel in a whiteout. "Better to stay put than get lost."

Well, normally he wouldn't have kept going, but it was easy to find Koyalik—just down the river.

Through the swirling curtains of white, Steve shouted encouragement to the dogs. "*Gih,* Mikki! Howler! Bandit! Bigfoot! Patch!" The sound of his own voice would have been reassuring except that it seemed to come from all directions at once.

They must be getting near Koyalik by now, but he could hardly see the river bank to tell.

Was the whiteout fading just a bit? Perhaps.

He slowed the dogs to a walk, steering them closer to the edge of the river, and Mikki swerved to avoid a pile of huge boulders.

Steve pulled on the brake, halted the team, and stared at the rock pile they had just passed.

There weren't any rocks near Koyalik. Not this pile of boulders.

This was Tall Rocks. He must have turned up the river by mistake. He felt as if an icy branch had hit him in the face. They were miles and miles from Koyalik.

The fog was definitely lifting, and through the falling snow he could see the cliffs and spruce trees that formed a sheltering canyon beside the river. Tall Rocks, for sure. He'd spent the night here on trips to Mierow Lake.

Okay, they'd take a rest, get something to eat, and turn back to Koyalik. Six hours at least. It was going to be a long day.

The dogs had dropped in their tracks and curled up with their backs to the wind, which seemed to be blowing colder by the minute. Maybe he could find the spot where they'd made camp last time.

He tramped up the river for a short distance, his snowshoes crunching on the snow-covered ice. A clump of ragged spruces stood nearby, with plenty of dead branches for firewood. Good.

His feet sank suddenly into knee-deep slush hidden beneath the snow. *Overflow.*

Instantly his feet and legs were soaking wet. Pain raced up his legs. He tried to step out of the water, and it felt as if he were lifting concrete pillars. With immense effort he dragged himself toward the trees. His snowshoes had turned to blocks of ice, and his feet were already beginning to stiffen.

If they froze, he was dead.

He dropped his mittens and fumbled with the icy bindings around his boots, but they resisted his gloved fingers. Wasting time. He pulled off his gloves and tore at the frozen rawhide with bare hands. His feet were going numb.

Finally he could kick the snowshoes off his boots. He stumbled toward a spruce tree and almost fell on his face. Hard to walk on those feet. He started off again, more careful of his balance. He staggered to the tree, pulled down two dead branches and ripped off twigs for kindling.

His hands were freezing fast. What about his gloves? No time. Pain raged through his legs, and his feet felt like nothing at all. Numb.

He tried to pull the matches from his pocket. *Fingers don't work.*

Using one hand as a claw, he jerked out the box of matches and it fell into the snow. With a cry, he dived after it. Couldn't let matches get wet. He clamped the box between his stiffened hands and clawed it open.

The long wooden matches lay there in neat rows—his ticket to warmth and life—but they looked impossibly small. He couldn't pick one up, not with these hands. His mind seemed to be turning to slush. What to do?

Teeth. Pick up a match with your teeth.

He used his left hand to beat his right hand into a tight fist, then put his face into the box and clamped a match between his teeth. Still using his teeth, he shoved one end of the match into his fist.

Now to light it.

He pushed the box closed and held it against himself with the useless left hand. He dragged the match in his fist across the rough side of the box.

It lit so suddenly that he let it fall to the snow.

Do it again. Hurry!

His hands were shaking with cold, but he finally lit another match and knelt to hold it close to the twigs. To his joy, the flame caught fire on the ragged ends of the twigs.

He bent close to shield the twigs from the wind and blew gently on the tiny fire. It flickered uncertainly, then grew, as one twig after another lit up.

The ruff of his parka was dangerously close to the flames, so he thrust his hood back with one arm. Cold air zinged across his head and face, but nothing mattered now.

Just another few minutes—to make sure those twigs were really burning. They flared up into his face, and he pushed the larger pieces of wood in close. Flames licked across them, and the dead wood lit with a reassuring crackle.

He jerked his hood back into place and held his freezing hands close to the fire, but a minute later he had to pull them away; he had burned a finger. After that, he warmed them more cautiously. Somehow he had gashed the top of one hand. It wasn't bleeding much, not in this cold.

He pulled his gloves on and tore at his boot laces, ripping off the icy boots and socks, then he held his feet as close to the fire as he dared. Tingling and prickling told him that the numbed flesh was coming to life, and he hastened the process by beating them with his hands.

As soon as his feet thawed, he yanked his fur mittens over them so he wouldn't have to walk barefoot in the snow. Then he hobbled back to the sled. He rummaged in his duffle bag to find the mukluks Liz had packed "just in case." Leaning against the sled, he pulled them on. They made his legs feel almost warm, and his feet sank into the soft dried grass inside. Never again would he tease her about "just in case."

Now for his axe. He chopped a good supply of wood and built up a roaring fire, trying to ignore the pain in his hands and feet. Pain meant life.

Next, the dogs and something to eat.

He hacked some good-sized chunks off a frozen caribou haunch and threw a piece to each dog. The last piece he roasted on a stick over the fire and ate it blackened on the outside, half raw inside. Not exactly tender, but the juicy red flesh tasted better than the most expensive steak he'd ever eaten.

Thank you, Lord, he thought automatically and realized with a jolt that all this time he hadn't even thought to pray.

He melted snow for the dogs and made tea for himself. What now? It seemed as if hours had passed, but pale twilight still hung behind the falling snow. It must be late afternoon. The dogs were rested, and Koyalik was straight down the river.

From the corner of his eye he glimpsed movement behind him. He glanced over his shoulder, and a gray shadow withdrew into the rocks. Might be better to head for home, rather than share a campsite with wolves. Besides, Liz would worry.

He put out the fire reluctantly, then packed up the sled and stepped onto the runners.

"*Gih,* Mikki. Take us home," he yelled, pedaling hard with his left foot to help break the frozen runners free.

Now that the immediate danger was past, his mind seemed to come unkinked. He had managed to get himself into serious trouble today. Why hadn't he made sure they turned the right way at the river?

For that matter, why had he kept going in a whiteout? He could have stopped and waited for it to pass instead of rushing ahead with what he wanted to do.

He watched the twilight darken. The storm seemed to be moving on. Perhaps there would be a moon so the dogs could see where they were going, but even without it, they seemed to instinctively avoid the danger spots. Like overflow.

Why hadn't he paid attention to where he was walking? He'd heard plenty about overflow—knew it was water that had forced its way up through the ice and turned to slush.

Knew it could be a death trap and was dreaded by the most experienced travelers.

He flexed his fingers, still painful in spite of the double warmth of gloves and mittens. And *why* hadn't he thought to put his gloves back on?

He'd panicked, that's why. Admit it. Some great out-doorsman, wasn't he?—proud of growing up in Minnesota, having his own dog team, knowing all the survival techniques. Well, he'd better learn some things fast if he was going to be a missionary in this wilderness.

He began to shiver, so he jumped off the sled to trot beside the dogs, but his accusing thoughts kept pace with him.

The missionary work wasn't going so well, was it? That Am-nok. He made you step back, didn't he? Interfered with your meetings, made a big impression on Charlie . . .

Charlie. He could see the boy's bright, enthusiastic face, his sparkling eyes. Something about that boy delighted him, made him want to be important to him. But compared to a shaman who could conjure up caribou, Steve Bailey didn't stand a chance.

Maybe he wasn't cut out to do this kind of work. Maybe, after all, he'd been kidding himself.

The thought lingered as the moon rose, giving occasional light between scudding clouds. The sound of far-off wolves blew across the tundra, and an hour later, he saw a straggling line of dark figures behind them on the ice. The dogs speeded up without urging, as if they did not like the idea of a wolf pack trailing them.

He dozed against the handlebars, listening to the rasp of the sled's runners over ice. Mile upon mile passed, and finally he saw lights in the distance. Cabin lights, from Eskimo homes on the far side of Koyalik's frozen lagoon.

He pulled himself out of a daze. There would be plenty to do now. Hungry families needed this meat.

They headed for the Trading Post, the dogs trotting wearily, panting clouds of frosted breath.

It looked as if Victor had arrived just before him because there was a crowd of Eskimos around his sled. Victor gave him a surprised glance as he drove up but did not say anything.

Steve helped to unload the meat from both sleds, then watched as Victor handed out caribou and received congratulations from the men who had gathered. In the fervent exclamations all around, he heard Am-nok's name more than once. From what he could tell, another party of hunters would set out at once to get the meat Victor had cached.

Steve recognized a few men who had come to church, and to them he said, "Isn't it wonderful how God answered our prayers? He gave us good hunting." They nodded and smiled in polite agreement, the way Eskimos always did. But what were they thinking?

Before long, the caribou meat was gone and only trampled snow remained in front of the Trading Post.

Victor packed up his sled with swift, efficient movements, then he glanced at Steve. "Bad storm. Whiteout. I just wait."

Steve could not bring himself to admit what had happened. "Yeah, bad." Victor would have built a cozy shelter of snow blocks and stayed put.

He clenched his aching hands inside his gloves, piled his share of the meat on the sled, and turned the dogs down the snow-packed lane.

Would Charlie count this as a victory for Am-nok?

Liz ran out of the cabin, pulling on her parka as she came. "You got caribou!" she cried. "I knew it when the children started yelling." Then she caught sight of the antlers on the sled and stopped short. "Oh! Can we keep them?"

"They're yours," said Steve. "But I gave your other present away."

She raised a questioning eyebrow.

"The tongue of my caribou. I let Victor take it to Nida."

She smiled, looking relieved. "Well, that's fine with me. Nida would know how to cook it anyway. Let me help you with the dogs. Poor things! They look starved." She knelt to give Mikki a welcoming hug.

Steve began unharnessing the dogs. "These poor things have been feasting on fresh caribou."

"How did they behave?"

"Pretty well, even Patch and Bandit."

Liz bent over the antlers, touching them gently. "So beautiful! I'll let you carry them inside while I go make some pancakes. Then after you unpack the meat, we can have a decent meal."

When he had finished with the dogs, Steve glanced at the sled. He'd unload that stuff later. He dragged himself into the cabin.

Just keep up a good face for Liz, he told himself. Maybe she won't suspect what happened. Or the way I'm feeling about this ministry.

He hung up his parka, and Liz came from the stove to give him a hug. He closed his eyes so he wouldn't have to meet her gaze.

"Steve!" She put a hand on his bruised shoulder, and he flinched. Her voice rose. "What happened to you?"

"What?" Why was she staring at him like that?

"Your eyebrows—they're singed. They're almost burnt off."

5 Tignak's Surprise

Steve dropped into a chair and rested his head in his hands. Should have known he wouldn't get away with it.

"And what about this?" She bent over the jagged cut on his hand.

"It's a long story, Lizzie," he mumbled.

"Okay." She backed away. "First we fix your hand, then you eat, then we'll talk."

After he'd cleared his plate of pancakes, fried Spam, and biscuits, Steve leaned away from the table.

Liz had eaten in silence, watching him. Now she poured him another cup of tea and looked expectant.

He started by describing the caribou hunt and how Victor had pushed him out of the bull's way.

"Vic was pretty casual about that." He took a drink of tea, wishing that was all that had happened. "But he sure was excited about finding the caribou. I wonder how much credit Am-nok will get."

"I wonder." Liz said. She seemed to know that there was more to tell.

Then he told her the rest, with all the details he knew she would want, not sparing himself; he included his agonized doubts on the way back.

"Something I realized too late," he said. "I never thought to ask the Lord for help. I was so scared that I forgot about Him."

Liz didn't look as if she thought what he'd done was so terrible. "But He remembered you. And He kept you safe—made you smart so you didn't freeze to death out there. Remember our verse—*Have not I commanded thee?*"

Steve looked at her in surprise. He'd forgotten that verse already, forgotten how the Lord had reassured him the night of the blizzard near Mierow Lake.

"Yes, I guess you're right." Something inside him thawed and melted. "Will you pray with me? I have some catching up to do."

After they finished, Liz went quietly to the stove and brought back a raisin pie. Steve smiled, but it wasn't because of the pie. "Now I know what I'm going to preach about on Sunday."

In the Sunday service, he preached from Psalm 46: *God is our refuge and strength, a very present help in trouble.* He told the small group about some of the things he and Liz had prayed for, and how God had answered. He emphasized how they'd prayed about the caribou and how thankful he was that God had showed Victor where to go.

"God takes care of His children," he said, looking into the unblinking black eyes. "When His children call to Him for help, He answers their cry. And even when they forget to call, He does not forget. He looks after them."

The expressions on the weather-beaten faces didn't change as Victor translated, and Steve wondered what he had told them.

Late the next afternoon as Steve walked home in the twilight, a dog team pulling a heavily loaded sled lumbered into Koyalik and slid to a halt.

At first he didn't recognize the short figure dressed in furs who stepped off the sled and waved at him. He shone his flashlight on the wrinkled brown face inside the fur ruff.

"Tignak!"

Behind Tignak came a second sled, driven by Charlie. The boy stopped his dogs and ran over to join them.

"Tignak, what's happening?" asked Steve.

"We've come to Koyalik. To live."

Steve stared at the two of them. He gripped Tignak's shoulder hard and grinned at Charlie. "That's wonderful news! Where will you stay? Never mind, my house is right down here. Come on in and we'll talk about it."

By the time the two dog teams had turned around and headed back toward Steve's cabin at the edge of the village, he was sure everyone was wondering about his visitors. The night was bitterly cold, so no one came out to ask questions, but they would be watching. What would they think when they saw Tignak walk into the white man's cabin that everyone was afraid to enter?

The little girl, Sarah, unrolled herself from a cocoon of caribou skins on Charlie's sled, and the bundle of furs on top of Tignak's sled turned out to be the grandmother. Liz came out to help the old Eskimo woman from the sled, but she slid down with practiced ease and walked stiffly inside.

Liz seemed delighted to have a houseful of visitors for supper. She settled the grandmother in a place by the stove, then she served up the caribou stew, talking nonstop to Sarah and Charlie as if they were her own family.

Their visitors ate in silence, obviously hungry after the long, cold journey. Steve told them about the caribou hunt. In conclusion, he said, "The people in Koyalik were getting pretty hungry. We prayed that God would send us some caribou, and I'm glad He did."

The grandmother smiled, her face a network of fine wrinkles. "Stew good." Tignak murmured in agreement, and Steve couldn't tell what he might be thinking. Charlie ate steadily, without comment.

After they finished, Steve said, "Tignak, I can't help wondering why you decided to come to Koyalik."

Charlie looked downcast as Tignak explained that he wanted his children to go to a good school. Besides, Koyalik was closer than Shanaluk to Tagatok, where his sister lived. He and Charlie would build a cabin. Until then, if there was no other place, they would live in a tent.

Liz poured more tea for everyone, and then Tignak asked whether there might be any empty houses in the village. "I saw one that looked deserted, over by the airstrip. But it has a padlock on the door. That's unusual."

"Yes, we've wondered about it," said Steve. "I heard that the cabin belongs to a white woman, but we've never seen her. A writer, I think Gus said. She visited a couple of villages on the coast last winter and is supposed to come back here some time. Anyway, you've got to stay here for now. And I'll help build your cabin if you don't mind unskilled labor."

He turned to Charlie. "There's good hunting around here. Those seals are going to howl when they hear that you've moved into town."

Charlie brightened. "Yes, I hunt seal! Maybe polar bear too." He joined happily in discussing plans for the new cabin. It would have four rooms instead of the usual one or two, and a wide storm porch in front. It would be built of spruce logs, of course, but Tignak would ask Gus to order some windows.

"Perhaps we could put it out here near your cabin," said Tignak, and Liz smiled in agreement.

Work began immediately. Steve went upriver with Tignak and Charlie the next day to find the trees they'd need for logs. They took a branch of the Tiskleet River that was new to Steve and followed it north until they reached the foothills of nameless mountains.

Tignak stood with his head thrown back to admire the towering spruce trees. "Now the work begins."

It was the hardest work Steve had ever done. Each day they left before dawn and raced up the river. Then they felled trees, cut and trimmed the logs, and hauled them by dog sled back to Koyalik.

Each night as he crawled into bed, aching in every muscle, he told himself that it was worth it. It was worth anything to have Tignak and Charlie here—and to get Charlie away from that shaman.

Soon, perhaps, Charlie would accept Christ. And maybe Tignak too, cynical though he might be.

The men of the village helped whenever they could, and out of necessity, Steve, Tignak, and Charlie sometimes took a day to go hunting with Victor or one of the other Eskimos. One memorable snowy afternoon, Charlie shot his first seal.

Tignak's family managed to fit themselves into Steve's cabin without difficulty. Tignak had stacked most of their belongings in the shed behind the cabin, since it had no storm porch. Steve took down the bookshelves and built makeshift bunks against one wall for the grandmother and Sarah. Tignak and Charlie slept on the floor by the stove. The only place left for their small table was in the center of the room, and even then, two people had to sit on a bunk in order to eat, but no one seemed to mind.

"Our cabin is looking more and more like a real native cabin," Steve said to Liz in a rare moment when they were alone. "We've got people sleeping on the floor, clothes strung on lines over our heads, and all kinds of stuff hanging on the walls."

She didn't seem concerned. "I feel like one of those old-time pioneer women—you know—'the table groaned under five different kinds of meat and vegetables and cakes and pies.' Only here it's caribou and boiled seal and dried salmon and seal oil with maybe some pickled wild greens."

"You're a good cook," said Steve. "And everybody liked that blueberry pie last night."

"You know what?" Her eyes were brighter than he'd seen them for a long time. "I think a few people have noticed that Tignak's family didn't die a terrible death from living under our roof. Yesterday Nida and two women came to visit. They actually sat down and drank tea with us."

"Gus told me it would happen someday, but I'm glad it's now," said Steve. "The Lord is doing wonderful things."

His gaze fell on the five red Bibles stacked on their bookshelf. Peter, the injured missionary who'd had to leave Koyalik, had sent those Bibles. Steve had plans for them. He was hoping to give one to Jackson, the pilot of the mail plane, and someday the others would go to four Christian Eskimos.

Immediately he thought about Tignak and Charlie. On Sunday, he'd watched Tignak's face while he preached. He and Charlie seemed to listen carefully, but it was a cumbersome way to speak, waiting for Victor to translate his message sentence by sentence.

"If only I could speak to these people in their own language!" He picked up his little Eskimo notebook. "I wonder if Tignak would teach us some Eskimo—really teach us—the grammar and how to write it and everything."

When Steve asked Tignak about lessons in Eskimo, the older man readily agreed. Every evening after that, Steve and Liz sat down with the lamp shining across their papers and did assignments under Tignak's watchful eye.

Steve found that Eskimo was a complicated language, just as Tignak had said. You couldn't string some words together and hope they'd make sense. There were dozens of word stems and endings that could change the meaning of a word. And a word might have a hundred different forms, depending on how it was used in a sentence.

One cold evening while Tignak and his family were visiting in another cabin, Steve took advantage of the quiet to work on their Eskimo dictionary. It was a good night to stay inside. Frost thickened on the windowpanes and gleamed from every nail head on the walls. He could hear the wind moaning and whining across Norton Sound.

"I just added six more words for 'snow' to our list," he said to Liz. "Six *different* words! We've got twenty-five words so far. That's incredible."

"You know what Tignak told me? They have only one word for 'flower.' There must be all kinds of flowers that bloom around here. One word! You can tell what's important to them."

"Like with Charlie. I suspect that he could learn to read dozens of new words each day if they had anything to do with hunting. How's he doing at school, by the way?"

Liz smiled. "Gus says he's catching on fast. He's starting to read on his own, but he's still pretty restless whenever he has to sit down at a desk."

"Poor kid! He sounds like me when I was his age. But he'll be glad someday." The wind howled around a corner of the cabin and made the stove pipe rattle. Steve got up to put some more wood on the fire.

When Charlie became a Christian, all that intelligence and energy could be directed towards something worthwhile, towards serving the Lord.

He picked up his pencil again. If he ever had a son, he'd want him to be something like Charlie.

Monday afternoon, Steve had just finished patching a hole in their stove pipe when the drone of an engine sounded overhead.

Charlie burst into the cabin. "Airplane! You say—"

"Right, let's go." Steve zipped up his parka and grabbed his heavy work gloves. "We can help him unload the plane. Coming, Liz?"

On their way down to the airstrip, Steve said to Charlie, "The pilot's name is Jackson. He's a great guy, a friend of ours. You ought to hear the stories he tells. You'll see he walks with a limp and has a scar on his face. Got those flying in the war. Gus said he has a box full of medals."

"You'll like Jackson," said Liz.

Charlie looked at Steve. "You fly planes too."

"Yes, how did you know?"

"Some kids talk how you fly sick man to Nome." He gave Steve an admiring glance. "You know lotsa things."

Steve smiled to himself and kept his eyes on the narrow, icy path that curved between the snowdrifts. Charlie seemed to be warming up.

He almost missed the boy's next question. "Kids tell me about another pilot. He crash."

"Yes, that was a friend of ours, Peter." He tried to explain about Peter's accident. "Peter was the first one to live in Koyalik and tell the people about God. He wanted us to come and help him, so we came. But one day a storm wrecked his plane."

"You so sad. He die?"

"No, but he was badly injured. Peter wants to come back to Koyalik someday."

"When you come here?"

"Last October," Steve said. How could so much have happened in just a few months?

Charlie grinned. "You still a *cheechako.*"

By the time they reached the airstrip, the plane had landed and the blond young pilot was unloading boxes and crates, stacking them on the snow-packed runway. A group of watchful children hung around, as usual, and several of the older ones were carrying boxes up to the Trading Post.

"Look at that," said Liz. "He's grown himself a mustache."

Jackson hauled out a pair of large suitcases, then glanced up and saw them. "Hey there! I was hoping you would come down. I have an interesting passenger today."

But Liz had already caught sight of the woman in the plane. She exclaimed in pleasure and hurried forward as Jackson opened the door of the cockpit.

The woman stepped down, ignoring Jackson's outstretched hand. She was a white woman, middle-aged, tall and dignified in her fur-trimmed parka.

Jackson gave them a lopsided grin that turned his mustache up at one side. "Folks, this is Mrs. Elsa Danner."

"Welcome to Koyalik," Liz said with her warm smile.

"How do you do?" The woman's voice was cool and light. She looked past Liz. "Jackson, I need these things taken up to my cabin right away."

6 That Danner Woman

Jackson raised an eyebrow, and Steve suspected that the mustache was hiding a smile. "At your service, ma'am."

Charlie jumped forward. *"Watzcookun!* I help too." He picked up a suitcase.

Steve and Liz exchanged an amused glance, then each took a suitcase and followed Elsa Danner away from the airstrip.

Steve looked back at Jackson, who was carrying three boxes and limping more than usual under their weight. The woman certainly had enough luggage. Maybe she was planning to stay for the rest of the winter. Liz would like that.

The lock on Elsa Danner's cabin door was an iron padlock big enough to chain a moose, and it was frozen solid. She turned to Jackson with an impatient exclamation, as if it were his fault. He ran back to the plane for a propane torch, and finally the lock thawed enough for her key to open it.

She put a shoulder to the door and pushed it inward. Together Steve and Liz took the suitcases inside.

The cabin was damp and cold, of course, but it was furnished as comfortably as any vacation cottage in the States. A Formica table and chairs. A shiny white stove. Shelves that obviously hadn't been made from wooden crates. Trim blue curtains at the windows.

He glanced at Liz, standing uncertainly at the door, taking it all in. It must look pretty luxurious to her.

"I can tell where these go," said Jackson. He lugged his boxes over to the bookshelves that stretched across one wall and dropped them with a thud.

Steve lit a fire in the stove, using some of the neatly stacked wood, and Elsa Danner sent Charlie outside to chop some more.

"I'll need two Eskimo women down here first thing tomorrow, Jackson," she said. "Hard workers, mind you, like the ones who worked for me last year. Need to clean this place up."

"Well," said Steve, "we'll be going. Nice to have met you, Mrs. Danner. Be sure to let us know if we can do anything to help."

Liz smiled and began to say something, but Elsa Danner was already opening the door. "I can cope. And I'm going to be very busy. I'm a writer, you know. Not much time for socializing."

"Goodbye, ma'am," said Jackson, sounding relieved.

Steve and Liz followed him out into the afternoon light that was already fading.

"Well, that's that, I guess," said Jackson. "She certainly hasn't changed much."

Liz gave him an inquiring look, and he added, "Flew her back and forth a couple of times when she was here last winter. She's not the sweetest person in the world." He brushed the ice crystals out of his mustache. "I'll go on up to the Trading Post. Have to talk to Gus."

Liz put a hand on the pilot's arm. "Can you stay for supper? It's too late to leave now, isn't it?"

"Not if I hurry, Liz. I'm sorry—real sorry! I haven't had a decent meal for a coon's age. But two weeks from now, let's see, that'd be Monday, the fourth of March, I'll be here for an overnight. How about then?"

"Good," said Liz. As Jackson turned toward the Trading Post, she laughed. "And take care of that mustache, okay? It makes you look older and more dignified."

"Yes, ma'am!" He gave them an embarrassed grin and hurried off.

During the next few days, the men pushed hard to get the walls of Tignak's cabin up before a major storm hit. By this time they had collected a good supply of logs, and it took shape rapidly.

Their own cabin bustled with people coming and going, preparing food and repairing tools, or eating, sleeping and reading, all done with a great deal of Eskimo and English chatter.

It seemed as if the grandmother was the only quiet person. She sat peacefully by the stove for hours at a time, but when Liz was working around the cabin, she helped in small ways. One day Steve heard Liz talking to her in jerky Eskimo. The old woman looked puzzled, then she said something in reply, and Liz began laughing.

Sarah fit in well with the other children at school and seemed to enjoy everything in her new life. She often stayed after school to help Gus in the small classroom or at the store.

Charlie's English was improving daily, although he didn't spend any more time at school than he had to. He helped with the cabin and the hunting and often did jobs for Elsa Danner. Tignak had sold one of his dog teams, but it was Charlie's responsibility to take care of the team that was left.

CHARLIE

He worked with Steve's dogs too, and he always gave special attention to Mikki.

One evening Tignak and Sarah went up to the Trading Post. Charlie didn't go, and Steve stayed in too, thinking this might be a chance to get to know him better. He told Charlie how Mikki had saved their lives on the trip to Mierow Lake, just a couple of months before.

The boy's eyes sparkled. "That Mik-shrok! *Wutz-buzin-cuzin!* I have to write story for school. I tell about Mik-shrok."

Liz set a pot of water on the stove. "Charlie, what was that strange word you used?"

The boy looked puzzled, then his face cleared. "*Wutz-buzin-cuzin.* You know it?"

The corners of her mouth turned up. "Oh, you mean, *What's buzzin', cousin?*"

Steve glanced up from sharpening his saw. "Where'd you ever learn an expression like that?"

Charlie looked knowing. "American kids come to Fairbanks. They say that. Like *watzcookun.*"

"Steve?" Liz smiled as she wiped off the table.

Steve put down the saw. "You're right, Charlie. But if you want to sound like the American kids, you've got to know when to say those expressions."

Charlie leaned forward. "Yes. When to ex-press?"

"Use them like a question, to ask what's going on," Steve said. "Or to say 'Hi, how're you?' "

"Okay," said Charlie. "What this one: *gimmesome skin?*" He frowned. "I know *skin,* but that other word—"

Liz almost dropped her dishcloth, laughing. "Give me some skin!" She picked up Charlie's strong brown hand, turned it over, and patted the skin on his palm. "It's for when you want to shake hands with someone."

"Okay!" Charlie jumped up. "*Gimme-some-skin!*" He shook hands with Steve, with Liz, and with the grandmother, then he grabbed his parka and danced out of the cabin.

Steve heard him outside, talking to the dogs. "*Watzcookun,* Bigfoot? Mikki, *Gimme-some-skin!*"

By the last week in February, Tignak's cabin was nearly finished. Wednesday night, the men worked late, but Steve had good news to share with Liz when he came in for supper. "Looks like the roof is done, at least for now. He'll have to wait until spring to put sod on it."

Steve picked up one of Liz's special butterscotch cookies on his way past the table. "These Eskimos are amazing. We need a window frame, see? So a man walks over and takes a look at the opening, goes off and cuts a piece of wood. It fits perfectly!"

He ducked under a line of drying clothes and sank into a chair, rubbing one shoulder. "Jackson should be bringing the windows in this week if the weather holds."

Liz was stirring something on the stove and seemed unusually quiet. "What's the matter, Lizzie? Oh, that Danner woman. You said you were going to make another try at visiting her."

"Didn't even get in the door," Liz said. "She told me— again—that she is very busy. But this time she accepted the cookies." She bent over the steaming pot, and Steve wished he could see her face.

"You'd think Elsa Danner would be glad to talk to you, even if she is writing a book or whatever it is," he said. "You're the only white woman for hundreds of miles around."

Liz shook her head. She seemed almost in tears. Steve crossed the distance to the stove in three strides and took her into his arms. "Don't let that woman get you down, Lizzie."

"It's not just Elsa Danner. I really wonder about Victor and Nida sometimes. Even though they let us have church at their house, I don't think they're really Christians . . ." Her voice trailed off, then it grew stronger. "And besides all that, I don't seem to have much of a ministry here. At least you get to preach on Sundays."

She gave him a faint smile. "This afternoon the Lord reminded me about our verse—you'd never know it by the way I'm behaving—but that helped a lot."

"Have not I commanded thee?" Steve held her tightly. "The Lord has sent us here, count on it," he murmured, reminding himself as well. "And He'll show us the best way to do His work."

"You're right." Her voice brightened. "Those antlers you brought me. I'd like you to put them on the wall by the stove."

"By the stove?"

"Yes. They'll be perfect to hang dishtowels and things on. Every time I see them, I'll remember our verse."

Charlie and Tignak came in for supper while Steve was nailing the antlers in place, and a minute later, Sarah arrived with the grandmother. While they ate, everyone discussed the new cabin, but Steve's thoughts wandered back to what Liz had told him about her visit to Elsa Danner that afternoon. Why was the woman so secretive?

He refilled Charlie's plate with stew and handed it to him. The boy was still doing odd jobs for Elsa Danner. Maybe he had found out something about her.

While Steve was trying to frame a question, Charlie stuffed a biscuit into his mouth and began talking about the woman. Today she had let him come into the cabin for the first time.

"Cabin real nice inside. Lotsa books. She write book about caribou." His eyes widened. "She have ears from caribou. And knife with handle that look like caribou foot. And head of caribou—all bones!"

Tignak shrugged. "A caribou skull would be useful to her. Gus told me she came back to do some more research, since Koyalik is pretty close to one of the caribou migration routes. From what he said, she was here last winter too, asking questions and buying things from the 'natives,' as she calls us. She's written other books—one about antelopes in some place like Africa. Seems to have plenty of money."

He split open his biscuit and gazed at it thoughtfully. "People around here don't think much of her, and the old ones are not happy to see her back. I don't think she is going to be good for our village."

Charlie's eyes narrowed to black slits, but he did not say anything.

Steve passed Tignak the pot of honey. Why had the boy been so impressed by a bunch of caribou bones?

That evening after everyone had settled down for the night, Steve tried to plan the service for Sunday, but his mind kept circling back to Tignak's remarks about Elsa Danner. None of the Eskimos, polite as they were, had said anything to him about the woman. But Tignak thought she was going to be a bad influence. Why?

She seemed to get along okay with Vic and Nida. She had hired Nida to cook for her, and she paid Victor well for taking her on trips up the river. Maybe it was because those two spoke a bit of English. But lately, Victor and Nida seemed to be changing.

The last time Steve and Liz visited the young couple, they had admired Nida's new chair, bought from a mail-order catalog. They had listened to Victor's hunting stories as usual, and they'd laughed together when Steve tried out some Eskimo sentences. But Victor hadn't said, "Come back, come back any time!" the way he used to. Something was different. Liz had felt it too.

I can't let this get me down, he thought. Where's that verse of ours? He opened his Bible to the book of Joshua and turned up the lantern.

He read the first few chapters of Joshua, thinking about the story there. It must have been a frightening time for Joshua. Moses had died, and now he had to take charge of this huge crowd of people who did a lot of complaining. God had told Joshua that it was time to move into the land, but right in front of them was a river in full flood and a fortified city named Jericho.

No wonder God had given Joshua this promise.

The lantern's glow highlighted the verse. *Have not I commanded thee?* And the next part said: *Be strong and of a good courage; be not afraid, neither be thou dismayed.*

Steve underlined the passage. Be not dismayed, huh? And Joshua *hadn't* been dismayed. He'd turned out to be a brave, courageous leader. How come?

Maybe because he'd remembered God's promise. And he'd depended on Him for courage.

Courage. Steve said it aloud. "Courage."

Liz looked up sleepily from the bunk where she was reading. "Courage?"

"That's what the Lord is going to give us, Lizzie, because I sure don't have any." He glanced at the antlers on the wall, hung with red-striped dishtowels, and smiled to himself.

Now he could think about Sunday. He opened his notebook and set to work.

The next day a letter came from Peter, who was living in San Francisco, and Steve read it aloud to Liz. Peter's enthusiasm seemed to crackle from each page: he was excited to hear about their experiences at Mierow Lake, he was fascinated by the story of Tignak, and he was praying for them day and night.

Almost as an afterthought, he mentioned that the doctor was going to operate on his leg one more time. Then they would tell him whether he'd ever be able to fly again. Meanwhile, he was praying that the Lord would provide them with a plane to help with the work, and he was writing to everyone on his prayer list about the tremendous needs in Koyalik, Shanaluk, and Mierow Lake. Even though he still had to use a wheelchair, he often spoke in churches, and he would ask them to pray about a plane too.

Liz took the letter from Steve to read for herself. After a minute, she said, "He's fighting the battle with us, isn't he? Think how much he'd love to be here too!"

She folded up the letter slowly, her eyes shining with determination. "You know what? I'm not going to wait any longer to start a Bible study for these kids. I'll call it our Story Club. Some of them can speak English, and most of them understand when I talk to them. Sarah! Where are you?"

The little girl looked down from her bunk. "Missus Lizzie?"

Liz jumped up and went over to whisper in Sarah's ear. A broad smile spread across Sarah's face, and she nodded vigorously.

After a long conversation, Liz came back to the table, smiling. "There, it's settled. Sarah wants to help me. We decided on Tuesdays and Fridays, after school. I'll talk to Gus about letting us use the schoolroom."

"Good idea!" said Steve. "The way those kids follow you around, it should be a great success."

He pulled a box out from under the table, looking for a pen and paper. He wanted to answer Peter's letter, and he really should write out a report for the Mission. But his mind swung back to Mierow Lake. Most of the Eskimos there spoke English, and they had welcomed his preaching on the last two trips. They'd learned some Bible verses and begged him to come back.

He listened for a moment to the wind blustering outside. Sure, the trip to Mierow Lake was long and dangerous in midwinter. But, like Liz, he wasn't going to wait any longer. He found a scrap of used paper in the box and began to make a list of supplies.

7 Icicles to Melt

By the first Saturday in March, Tignak's house was finished. Eskimo fashion, he invited the whole village to come for a feast.

In the largest room stood two tables covered with oilcloth and piled with food. Besides plenty of walrus, seal, and caribou, there were half a dozen pies that Liz and Sarah had made, and many Eskimo delicacies such as *muktuk,* which was raw whale skin and blubber.

Even Gus came. It was the first time Steve had seen the old trader at a party, but he seemed right at home. The Eskimos were having a wonderful time eating, telling jokes, and swapping stories, and Gus strolled from one group to the next. When the feasting was well underway, Steve and Liz joined him in a less noisy corner where, plate in hand, he was studying Tignak's new bookshelves.

"Looks like everyone showed up," Gus said, nodding at the crowd. "Except that Danner woman."

Liz nibbled at a piece of dried salmon. "She certainly was invited."

"I don't think she's very fond of Eskimos," Gus said thoughtfully. "Yah, she can't understand their language, so she calls it gibberish."

"It's the most complicated gibberish I've ever seen," Steve said, "and I studied Greek and Hebrew at school."

"You're doing pretty well. Took me years to learn it. Even so, I still wonder if they go home and laugh among themselves at the funny way I talk."

Gus looked at the tables of food. "I'm going to get me some more of that pie, then go watch the dancing. By the way, Elsa Danner was pestering me with some more of her endless questions, and for once she unbent far enough to ask about you two. Sounds like she's curious."

After Gus left, Liz said, "Jackson's coming for supper Monday night. I wonder if Elsa Danner might want to join us."

"Wouldn't hurt to invite her," Steve said. "Maybe she'll be curious enough to come look us over."

"What's going on back there?" asked Liz. Men had cleared the furniture out of one of the back rooms, and drums were beginning to beat softly.

"Let's go see."

Three men stood against the back wall, beating drums made of driftwood and walrus skin. A growing circle of by-standers chanted a monotonous, incomprehensible song. In the center of the room, a man moved into a series of grace-ful poses, and Steve soon realized that he was telling a story.

Keeping time with the drums, the man portrayed a hunter stalking a seal. Vividly, he was the seal, then he was a hunter peering across the ice. The whole scene came to life: the cold, the broad white expanse of ice, the sleeping seal.

"Beautiful!" whispered Liz.

In the next story, a hunter slipped stealthily among the icebergs, following a polar bear.

Steve gazed at the bystanders, who watched the story-teller with delighted faces. What a difference it would make if a dozen of them would come to church tomorrow and be as responsive as this crowd!

He had to think of some way to put more life into the Sunday service. People didn't seem to connect with what he was trying to say. Did they come just to be polite?

It was late when they finally left Tignak's cabin, and Steve's head pounded with the noise of the drums, but after they had done the usual bedtime chores, he asked Liz to pray with him about tomorrow's service.

"Why don't we teach them a song?" she asked. "Something like 'Heavenly Sunlight.' These long dark days get me down, and I know everyone is glad to see the sun for a few more minutes each day. It's a cheering song."

"Okay." Steve whistled the song. "It has some good words too. Wish we could teach it in Eskimo. Maybe Victor can explain it, and then I'll use that to introduce my message."

Sunday morning, besides Victor's and Tignak's families, six other people came to Victor's cabin for the service. To start off, Steve and Liz sang "Heavenly Sunlight" for them. Then Steve asked Victor to translate the English into Eskimo while they sang it again, one line at a time.

Walking in sunlight, all of my journey,
Over the mountains, through the deep vale;
Jesus has said, "I'll never forsake thee,"
Promise divine that never shall fail.

The grandmother, sitting in the front row, lifted her head. She leaned forward, her face shining, and murmured something in Eskimo.

"She know that song," said Charlie, beside her.

Steve stopped in the middle of a line. "Ask her if she'll sing it for us."

Charlie translated the request, and the old woman began to sing in a cracked, wavering voice that grew stronger and stronger. The words certainly were Eskimo, long, rhythmic, and impossible for Steve to follow, and she had the tune perfectly.

"*Kuyana!* Thank you!" he exclaimed when she finished. Then, in careful Eskimo, he asked, "Will you teach us?"

Her face broke into a hundred smiling wrinkles as she nodded. Slowly she led the small group through the song, and then once again. The squirming children joined in, and even the babies stopped crying. By the third time, everyone had learned it, and the cabin rang with their enthusiasm.

Steve stood up to preach, thankful for the song. "We all know about journeys over mountains," he began. "And even with my good dogs, I don't like to travel when it's dark." He held up his open Bible and talked to them about God's promises. Victor translated as usual, and for once, Steve felt as if the small audience heard what he was trying to say.

But after everyone had left, Victor turned to him, and a shadow on the young Eskimo's face warned that something was wrong.

"Good service," Victor said. "Soon lotsa people come."

"I hope so." He waited, knowing that Victor would get to the point sooner or later.

Victor gazed about the room, not meeting Steve's eyes. Finally he said, "I think our house too small. Maybe you have church somewhere else?"

"Your house is just fine," Steve said. "I'm very happy to use it."

Victor was silent, looking uncomfortable.

"But if the meeting makes it too crowded for you . . ."

"Yes, yes, too crowded," said Victor hastily. "My children getting big. My wife, she think too many people here all the time."

But Victor's wife loved nothing more than a crowd of people. Steve tried to smile. "Well, in that case, we'll find some other place. People don't mind coming to my cabin now, so maybe that would work."

Victor nodded and smiled. "So far so good." He busied himself with putting wood into the stove, and Steve went to find Liz, who was still talking to one of Victor's children.

He put a hand on her shoulder. "Time to go, Lizzie." He picked up his parka and headed out the door.

Liz caught up with him a few minutes later. "You sure left all of a sudden. The sermon went well today, didn't it? I'm so thrilled that Grandmother knew our song. That made all the difference. I'll have to find out how in the world she learned it."

"Yeah." But what had happened to Victor? He and Nida had been having the church services in their cabin right from the start, when Peter was here. They always seemed delighted when people came.

"What's the matter, Steve?"

He told her what Victor had said, and she scuffed through the snow in silence. Then she said, "Something's wrong with those two. I wonder what it is."

Steve didn't want to think about that. Victor was his friend. Victor and Nida had been their only encouragement in Koyalik. Suddenly everything in the little village seemed distasteful. He eyed the banks of snow that rose on either side of the path. It was dirty snow, stained with blood from the last seal hunt and littered with wood scraps, bones, and discarded tin cans. "Maybe it'll snow," he said. "Cover up all this stuff."

Liz gave him a puzzled glance. "I thought you were planning a trip to Mierow Lake. Last night you were hoping we wouldn't get another storm for a long time."

"Yeah." Steve tried to shake off his discontent. "I've got to go to Mierow Lake. I was going to ask Vic to come along. I know you can't leave your Story Club. But now this! I guess there's no reason why I can't go alone."

Liz stopped short. "Alone? You can't go alone! You know what Gus would say."

"Yes. He'd say I'm crazy. So maybe I am." Steve kicked a soup can out of his way. "Don't worry about it. I've got a strong team, and Mikki is almost as good as another person."

Liz looked unconvinced, but she started walking again. "I think we ought to do a bunch of praying about this."

Monday afternoon, Steve talked to Gus about supplies for his trip to Mierow Lake but didn't mention that he was planning to go alone. Charlie was already in the store, studying the knives in a glass case under the counter. Gus went back into the storeroom to get him a coil of new rope, and Steve looked up to find Charlie standing beside him.

"You take trip with dogs?" the boy asked. "You let me come too?"

A warmth spread through Steve's chest, but he shook his head. "Better not. You'd miss a whole week of school." He thought about how much he'd like to have the boy along. "But ask your father. Maybe, if it's okay with him . . ."

Charlie's dark eyes gleamed, and he headed for the door as if he were going to track down his father that very minute.

Gus came back with the rope and handed it to Steve. "That's the last rope I have for a while. Don't let those dogs of yours chew up any more." While Steve was paying him, the trader said, "I heard that your wife finally talked Elsa Danner into coming over for supper. That's an event worth noting!"

Steve grinned. "Word sure gets around fast. I hope we can melt some of those icicles. Jackson will be there. That'll help. Oh, that reminds me. I was supposed to ask you for some walnuts."

That evening, precisely at six o'clock, Steve knew by the dogs' howling that someone was coming up the path. A minute later, Elsa Danner knocked on his door.

Jackson, who had come early, stood up. "She knocks, even. Anyone else would've just walked in." He went with Steve to the door.

Elsa Danner stood in the doorway, letting icy air blow inside. She finished brushing the snow from her mukluks and gestured over her shoulder. "That dog of yours. He looks like a wolf."

From where he was chained to the side of the cabin, Mikki stared at her. He opened his mouth wide, showing impressively sharp teeth, and yawned a cloud of frosted breath.

"Mikki? I guess he has some wolf in him," said Steve. "A lot of dogs around here do."

She stepped inside. "This village seems to be full of wolf-dogs. That one's the worst. And I don't like the way he looks at me."

Liz joined them, smiling. "I'm glad you could come, Mrs. Danner. You remember Jackson, don't you?"

Elsa Danner's gaze flicked over the tall blond pilot. "Yes, I do," she said. "Did you get my telegram sent from Nome?"

"Yes, ma'am. I certainly did." Steve smiled to himself at the twinkle in Jackson's blue eyes.

"Good." The woman began to take off her parka and Steve stepped forward to help her. She wore her caribou skins with grace, and her blond hair was pulled into an elegant knot at the back of her head.

Liz carried a plate of roasted potatoes to the table. "Everything's ready," she said. "We can sit right down."

Now that Tignak's family had moved out, all four of them could sit at the table. Liz had put out their best plates, Steve noticed. And she had made Jackson's favorite—lima beans with bacon.

After Steve asked the blessing, Liz went to the stove and returned with a platter of sizzling caribou steaks. "I hope you like caribou, Mrs. Danner," she said brightly.

"Of course. What else is there to eat in this barbaric country? I've learned to like it, along with moose and seal and muktuk." She paused, looking pained. "But I refuse to eat rabbit."

"Pretty tough, sometimes," Steve said. "But Liz has this stew she makes—"

"It's not the taste. It's the look in their eyes."

"I know what you mean," Liz said. "I used to have a pet rabbit when I was a girl, and I threatened to leave home when they started talking about fried rabbit."

Elsa Danner favored her with a nod and sawed a small piece off her steak. She chewed it in silence, darting glances around the room. Her gaze lingered on the rack of caribou antlers, hung with towels and mittens, then moved to the shelves of books.

"Well, you have more books than I've seen for a while," she said. "And a whole stack of Bibles? You'll never get anyone in this village to read one."

"A few people are learning English," said Liz. "And Gus is doing a good job at the school." She smiled. "We'll use those Bibles someday."

Steve nodded. "Someday. In the meantime, I sure wish we had something written in Eskimo that we could use with them."

Elsa Danner shrugged, and Liz got up to bring more food from the stove. Steve refilled their mugs with tea.

Jackson ate with the single-mindedness of a man who enjoys his food. Finally, after his second helping of steak, potatoes, lima beans, and stewed tomatoes, he spoke. "I hear you're learning some Eskimo, Steve."

"Yes, Tignak is a good teacher, and it's finally beginning to make some sense to me."

"Why are you learning Eskimo?" asked Elsa Danner.

"We're here because we want to teach the Eskimos about God," Steve said. "They'll understand us better if we can speak their language."

"Hmm." She frowned. "They're such a backward people, intellectually speaking. Don't you think you're wasting your time? And superstitious! I was doing research in a village down the coast, and with a bit of fast talking, I convinced them that I could speak to the Spirit of the Sea. Then

I presented a necklace of seal claws to the headman's wife, and after that, I had them eating out of my hand."

Abruptly she turned to Jackson. "I hear wolves howling at night, more than last year. Do you think they've got dens up the river somewhere?"

"I doubt it," said Jackson. "The caribou have shifted their route and the wolves are probably following them."

"Are you studying wolves for your book?" asked Liz.

Elsa Danner straightened. "My book is about *caribou*," she said with disdain. "One of the most majestic and powerful creatures on the face of the earth. And useful too! If it weren't for them, the natives would have died out long ago."

She glanced at Steve. "Have you ever seen a young bull with a magnificent set of antlers still in velvet? Or watched a thousand caribou race through a valley at full gallop?" Her face softened. "I have. I'll never forget it."

Liz leaned forward, looking fascinated, and the woman seemed to remember her question. "But those wolves," she said sharply, "they're a menace to all wild game. This year the caribou population is down because the wolves have taken over the tundra. I certainly approve of using poison on them—that's an excellent idea the government came up with. I wouldn't mind helping them out myself. The wolves should be destroyed."

Jackson rubbed at the scar on his face. "Well, now, that's the current theory, but the game population has managed itself just fine for hundreds of years. Why interfere?"

A spot of red burned in each of Elsa Danner's cheeks. "How can you say that?" she exclaimed. "Wolves kill caribou by the hundreds, just for the fun of it. And they've been known to attack people too."

"You'll hear stories like that," said Jackson mildly. "I call it the Red Riding Hood myth—wolves are pictured as snatchers of grannies and small children—but there's no proof. On the other hand, a lot of people will argue that the wolf is a useful creature. There's plenty of evidence that wolves keep the herds in good condition by killing the weak and sick caribou, for instance."

He took a drink of tea and smiled at her over the rim of his mug. "I think we forget that wolves are not people. They're animals. They're predators. They're made to kill other animals."

"They're murderers." Elsa Danner stabbed at the last piece of meat on her plate and shook her head. "I hate them," she muttered. "If I could, I'd get rid of every single wolf in Alaska."

8 For Good Hunting

The next evening, when Steve and Liz had grown tired of practicing Eskimo verbs, Tignak mentioned the trip to Mierow Lake. "Charlie's been begging me to let him go."

"I didn't think you'd want him to miss school," said Steve.

"That's true. But a trip like this might be good. I worry about him. He didn't want to move here, and I'm not sure he's changed his mind."

"He seemed to be fascinated by that shaman back in Shanaluk," said Steve.

The wrinkles across Tignak's forehead deepened. "Yes, that's one reason I wanted to move. But now he's got this idea that Elsa Danner has some kind of connection with the spirits—just because of the dried-up bones and carvings on her shelf. And the caribou ears. Those are thought to be a powerful amulet."

Liz gave him a questioning look. "Amulet?"

"A charm, you might call it. According to the old Eskimo beliefs, if you carry a small object like a carving of a whale or the teeth of a bear, the spirit of that animal will protect you or give you good hunting or whatever. The ears of the caribou are supposed to make the wearer quick of hearing. Many Eskimos carry amulets. The more the better, they think."

"Do you believe that?" asked Liz softly.

"Me?" Tignak ran a hand through his thinning black hair. "Well, there's no scientific proof that amulets work. I don't know what I believe. Anyway, the other day Charlie went out hunting on the ice. The weather was bad, but he was determined to get a seal."

"We've got plenty of food," said Steve. "Why'd he go?"

"That's what I asked him. Finally he told me that the Danner woman had asked him to bring her the teeth and claws of a seal. He's hoping she'll use them to make an amulet for him."

Steve clenched his hands around his mug. Like the seal-claw necklace she'd boasted about. That woman! "I'm worried about Charlie," he said.

Tignak looked down at the table, but not before Steve had glimpsed the pain in his eyes. "You pray for him. Maybe it will help."

Steve gazed at the old Eskimo. Tignak needed the Lord too. Somehow, this didn't seem like a good time to go off to Mierow Lake and leave him.

"You wouldn't want to come to Mierow Lake with me, by any chance?"

The weathered face brightened. "Sure would. Haven't had a good long dog sled trip for a while. We can take Charlie, and I'll make sure he stays caught up with his schoolwork."

Steve exchanged a smile with Liz and silently thanked God.

The next day, he made arrangements for being gone during the next week or so. Liz would keep an eye on the grandmother and Sarah, and together they would continue with the Story Club.

Surprisingly enough, Victor offered to have the church service at his cabin while Steve was away. The young Eskimo looked so apologetic that Steve felt sorry for him.

He went up to the Trading Post for a few last items, and while he was talking to Gus, he shared his worries about Victor and Nida.

Gus listened, stroking his neat gray beard. "Yah, I think it's that Elsa Danner. She's an odd one. She talks against you—that you are going disrupt the Eskimo way of life. Apparently she doesn't think much of missionaries."

"I got that impression," said Steve. "But I'm still hoping she'll change her opinion of us."

He tried to dismiss the thought of Elsa Danner, but even while he was checking his supplies and packing the sled, she remained an unwelcome presence in his mind. At least, this trip would take Charlie away from her.

They left early Thursday morning, traveling in the faint golden light of sunrise. Charlie trotted beside Tignak's sled, singing to the bright sky. The dogs skipped and pranced with excitement, even Mikki, who was supposed to set a good example.

Steve drew in great tingling breaths of the icy air, glad for the lengthening days, glad for the prospects of this trip with Tignak and Charlie.

The sleds skimmed over the well-traveled ice, accompanied by the squeak of runners and softly thudding paws, and after the first hour, the dogs settled down to a steady lope that ate up the miles.

They reached the Big Rocks campsite before sunset, in plenty of time to do some hunting. The clump of ragged trees still stood on the spot where Steve had been so cold, so afraid, just a few weeks before. He drove the sled quickly past, toward the sheltering cliffs.

Tignak decided that he would rig the tent while Steve and Charlie hunted rabbits for supper.

They took their guns and tramped through the snow toward the jumble of rocks and underbrush that bordered a frozen creek. Charlie's face glowed, his energy still running high, even after a day of mushing. He paused by a pile of boulders and studied the clumps of brush. One hand moved to clasp something that hung from a string around his neck.

Steve watched him holding the amulet, and the boy must have felt his gaze.

"For good hunting." Charlie opened his mittened hand wide enough for Steve to see the sharp, curved claws of some kind of bird.

"Where'd you get them?"

A snowshoe rabbit, almost invisible against the white, drifted past them. Charlie raised his rifle and fired in one smooth motion.

The rabbit jerked and fell over. Charlie was upon it right away with his knife, quickly slitting down the belly to gut it. As Charlie worked over the rabbit, Steve saw another one, fired, and brought it down too.

Charlie wiped his hands clean on the snow and pulled on his mittens. He looked fondly at the dangling claws. "Am-nok, he get this for me. Owl good hunter. Owl spirit help me when I hunt."

Am-nok, thought Steve. Of course.

His hands were numb with cold and he hurriedly pulled his mittens back on.

They followed a promising set of tracks for a short distance down the creek, then waited again in the fading light. The cold crept through Steve's caribou furs and tingled down his back, but he stood still, as still as Charlie. Finally each of them shot another rabbit, and they turned back toward the camp.

"Those owl claws," said Steve. "How can you tell for sure that they help you?"

"Lotsa times I have good hunting when I hold them. Am-nok, he know all about spirits. He tell me." Charlie's voice drifted away, as if he were remembering some mystical experience.

A rabbit dashed by, almost underfoot. Steve fired, and his bullet puffed harmlessly into the snow. Charlie fired, and the rabbit ran two steps farther, trailing blood, then dropped.

To his credit, the boy said nothing, but after he'd gutted the animal, he picked it up by its hind legs and swung it triumphantly in the air. He chattered all the way back to the campsite, and Steve felt a crushing weariness.

Tignak had finished setting up the camp site. Steve stood close to the blazing fire and warmed his hands while

Charlie told his father about the hunt. Neither of them mentioned the amulet.

Soon the rabbits were frying, giving out a mouth-watering smell, and the bannock that Liz had sent was toasting beside them. Charlie grinned broadly when he found a packet of cookies in the food box.

They ate in comfortable silence, hunched close to the fire, and watched the moon rise over the dark pointed tips of the spruce trees.

From somewhere nearby came the *whoo, hoo, hoo* of an owl, and Charlie gave a low exclamation of delight. Tignak looked at him, his wrinkled face thoughtful, but all he said was, "Snowy owl. They call him the ghost of the Arctic."

They lingered with their tea as the fire burned lower and lower. Steve was beginning to think about his warm sleeping bag when Charlie jerked upright.

"Behind you," he whispered to his father. "Wolf shadow in rocks." He reached for his rifle.

"Let him be," said Tignak.

The boy's hand lingered on his gun. "Mrs. Danner say—"

"I know what Mrs. Danner says." Tignak's voice deepened. "Let him be. I don't want to stop and skin a wolf carcass now. And I do not agree with Mrs. Danner's opinion of wolves."

The old Eskimo kicked the embers of the fire together and flames blazed up, enough for Steve to see the rebellion on Charlie's face. The boy put down his gun.

Tignak smiled at him and then at Steve. "As Victor likes to say, 'So far, so good.' Better get some sleep. Tomorrow we'll be traveling on the Yukon, and that's no picnic."

9 One Smart Cookie

Steve was awakened the next morning by such a confusion of clucking, chuckling, and calling that he thought, hazily, that the tent must be surrounded by a flock of chickens.

Charlie was already on his feet, snatching up his rifle, and crawling silently to the tent flap.

In a few minutes there came loud cackling and rifle shots. Then he returned, grinning, with a couple of ptarmigan. The small birds made for an excellent breakfast, along with hot oatmeal and bannock spread with jam.

They hitched up the dogs and set off again, turning onto the broad Yukon River, which meandered north between low foothills. Before long, the wind rose, scooping away the snow and scouring the river ice until it was bare and slick.

Tignak shouted to Steve, looking grim. "Glare ice!"

The dogs flattened themselves and spread their legs, trying to get some traction, and the sleds began to swerve. Steve stood with both feet on the brake, but its teeth merely scratched the ice, and his sled skittered forward until it rammed against a snow bank several yards downstream. Time after time, he lost control of the sled, and once, to his and Mikki's frustration, the sled went round in a full circle.

The dogs whined in complaint, and it was slow going for several hours. Finally the river twisted between islands that blocked the wind, and Charlie, looking ahead of them, sent up a shout. "Snow here on ice!"

Tignak called a rest stop, and they pulled onto a gravel bar to make hot drinks and water the dogs. When the dogs had rested enough to start fighting with each other, they set off again. For several miles, they trotted in peace, and Steve was daydreaming about the kind of airplane he'd like to buy when Mikki lurched off the river ice and churned up the bank into drifted snow.

What was the matter with him?

Steve ran to the front of the team and grabbed Mikki's collar, meaning to turn him back.

Tignak shouted to get his attention. He had halted his team at the point where Mikki left the ice, and now he commanded his leader to lie down.

The old Eskimo took his axe from the top of his load and walked ahead of the dogs, using the axe handle like a blind man's cane, tapping before each step.

Two yards farther, ice crackled—Steve could hear it from where he stood—and a line of gray spread out before them.

Overflow.

Apparently the band of dangerous slushy ice stretched all the way across this channel of the river, and Tignak ordered his team up onto the bank too. The snow was so deep that they had to help the dogs, pushing the sleds through drifts for what seemed an endless distance. Finally Tignak checked the ice again, and they floundered back down onto the river trail.

Steve roughed up the thick gray fur on Mikki's neck. "Good boy," he said. "Someday I'll learn to listen to you."

"That Mik-shrok," exclaimed Charlie, looking pleased. "He one smart cookie, yes!"

They left the Yukon for another river that twisted toward the mountains and became narrower with each mile. When dusk began to fall, they were in a spot encircled by mountains, with wooded hills rising directly from the edge of the river.

There was no convenient gravel bar to camp on, but Tignak pointed out a small open space back among the trees, so they left the sleds on the river and humped their supplies up the steep bank.

Together Charlie and Steve took the dogs, one by one, up to the campsite and chained them to trees at the edge of the clearing. As they were walking back toward the fire, a small white animal crossed their path and vanished into the darkness.

"Ahh . . ." Charlie stopped to gaze after the fox. His hand closed over a carved ivory figure that hung from his parka. "Am-nok make me fox amulet," he said with satisfaction. "Fox never afraid. Fox fast and smart. Pretty soon I get seal claws too. Mrs. Danner fixing for me. Then I be good hunter on ice too."

Steve groaned aloud. "Charlie, just think about it for a minute." He faced the boy. "You're already a good hunter. You're smart, you have sharp eyes, and you're getting more experienced every day. There's nothing that woman can do to help you shoot seals or anything else. She's just pretending so you'll do what she wants."

Charlie lifted his chin, his lips in a stubborn twist. "*Eeelai!* You hate her, yes!" Before Steve could answer, he exclaimed, "She know more about caribou than Am-nok. She talk to those bones. That skull. Sometime she learn things from spirits. She tell me." His voice broke, and he turned away.

Steve followed, an icy weight settling on his shoulders. Even when he finally crawled into his sleeping bag and tried to relax in its soft warmth, Charlie's words tramped coldly through his mind. *"You hate her, yes!"*

Tignak awoke them at dawn, and through the haze of his exhaustion, Steve heard him saying something about deep snow.

After they had traveled a few miles, Steve understood the old Eskimo's concern. Since the last time he was here, a huge amount of snow had fallen. Soon they would have to leave the river and cross the mountains.

He found the red-streaked rocks that marked the turnoff, but there was no sign of the trail he'd used before. He guided the teams off the river in what he guessed was the right direction, and immediately the dogs were up to their shoulders in soft snow. Steve got behind his sled and pushed, and the dogs fought their way forward. Tignak and Charlie did the same.

Whenever the team bogged down completely, Steve stepped to the front of the sled and gave the towline a sharp, quick tug, pulling the team back so they instinctively leaped forward. Even so, the trip became a series of stops and starts, with longer and longer stops for the tiring dogs.

Finally the men had to take turns leading the way, stamping down the snow with their snowshoes to break a trail. They labored up one ridge and down the next, up again and down, through one spruce forest after another.

Hours passed, exhausting hours marked by clouds of frozen, panting breath, aching legs, and numbed fingers.

Steve kept his eyes open for the huge uprooted tree that he used as a landmark and found it, half-buried in snow, near the top of the last ridge.

"Almost there!" he exclaimed.

They made a fire and took another rest stop. Each of them leaned against a tree, wordless, to drink a mug of strong tea.

The hot, sweet liquid felt good going down, and it warmed Steve to cheerfulness. Not much longer now.

He looked at Charlie and gestured across the rolling expanse of snow-crowned trees. "Remember how I told you Mikki saved our lives? Somewhere out there is the place we camped that night in the blizzard."

Charlie's eyes gleamed. "What a dog!"

"You said it. God gave us a great blessing when He gave us Mikki."

Charlie looked thoughtful, as if he hadn't expected such an answer.

Tignak was squinting down at the long valley. "There's the lake."

"Yes, and somewhere along here they usually have a decent trail down to the village." Steve tramped along the ridge until he reached a wide, hard-packed path, obviously well-used. "Here it is. My dogs like to run down this slope so fast, I'm sure I'll break a leg some day."

Steve had wondered whether the people at Mierow Lake would remember him—it had been almost two months—but he stopped wondering right away. Before their sleds were halfway through the village, men and women and dozens of children ran out of the cabins to greet them.

One of the first was a tall man with thoughtful black eyes. It was Samson, the man who had learned the Bible verses from Liz's picture book. Samson helped them chain and feed the dogs. Other men unpacked the sleds and carried supplies into the small cabin that was kept for Steve's use.

Soon they had been invited to eat supper at the Nanouk home. Jacob and Mary Nanouk, plump and smiling, were the young couple who had come to ask questions on his last trip. He was glad to introduce them to Tignak and Charlie.

They stayed for three days. Steve preached twice each day, and Tignak translated into fluent, expressive Eskimo. Even though most of his audience knew English, they seemed to appreciate hearing their own language. Many, particularly the Nanouks, stayed after the services to talk to him and ask about life in the States.

Apparently they had heard the gospel before, and many of them talked as if they were Christians. But something troubled Steve about the questions they asked. Even Jacob and Mary Nanouk seemed to want a set of rules to follow, and not much more.

On the last night, as they were packing their gear, Tignak said, "You don't seem to be especially happy, Steve. These people think you are wonderful."

"That's just it. They're thinking about me, the white missionary. They're not thinking about Jesus Christ. They don't realize that they need Him . . ."

He gazed at the skillet he had picked up, and shook his head. Tignak didn't realize his need of Christ either, so he wouldn't understand.

Silently he packed up the cooking pots and stashed their dwindling supply of food in the canvas bag, leaving out the skillet and a few things for breakfast.

Tignak was sewing a strip of caribou hide onto a broken harness. "What did Samson ask you after the service tonight?"

"He asked me to write down some prayers for him to use while I'm gone."

"What's wrong with that? Lots of religions use prayer formulas."

Steve glanced at Charlie. The boy was leaning against the table, drinking cocoa. "It all comes back to knowing Jesus Christ. If a man belongs to Christ, he can talk to God as his heavenly Father, naturally, from his heart."

Tignak nodded politely, but Steve could tell that it didn't make much sense to him. And Charlie didn't seem to be listening.

He unrolled his sleeping bag on the floor and sat on it to take off his mukluks. "But at least they're interested. And hearing the Eskimo from you was important. Charlie's been a great help too, taking care of the dogs and all."

He looked at the two of them, one old and one young, thinking what good friends they were. "You know, God has given me and Liz a verse from the Bible that's sort of our own special verse. When I get discouraged, I try to remember it: *Have not I commanded thee? Be strong and of a good courage; be not afraid, neither be thou dismayed.*"

Again Tignak nodded without saying anything, and Charlie yawned.

Steve jerked off his second mukluk. Oh well, it was late. Time to stop talking and get some sleep.

They started early the next morning, zigzagged up the ridge, and then looked for the trail they had worked so hard to make. Steve was relieved to find that it was still passable. Wind had coated the snow with a two-inch crust, and the sleds moved easily over the top without breaking through to the powder beneath.

When they reached the river, they found that the ice was covered with new snow, so the dogs had plenty of traction, and they made good time.

For the last day of the trip, they were slowed by a wind that seared their noses and chins with cold and kicked whirling clouds of snow into the air. But the dogs were headed for home and they knew it. "There's no stopping them!" yelled Charlie.

Let them run, thought Steve. I can't wait to get home either.

Liz was full of news. Two families had come to Victor's cabin for the church service. She hadn't seen anything of Elsa Danner. Three new children had showed up at Story Club. Sarah was learning English remarkably fast.

While he unpacked, Liz told him that she'd talked to the grandmother several times, and she was sure the old woman was a Christian. Apparently, long ago she had gone to a missionary's school, somewhere up north.

"It's such a happy thing to find out." Liz shook her head, smiling. "Now we pray together every day."

She wanted to hear all about the trip. When Steve told her about his conversations with Charlie, she exclaimed, "Oh, that boy!" and looked as downcast as he felt. Then, with her usual brightness, she added, "But let's keep praying for him and Tignak. I just know the Lord is going to do something wonderful for them."

That night, snug under furs on their bunk, Steve listened to the comfortable sound of wood crackling in the stove and thanked God for His protection on the long trip. Rumbling thunder, punctuated by loud booms, came from the pack ice out on the ocean where the wind was shifting and crushing the ice. They had come back just ahead of another storm.

By morning, the noise of the pack ice was lost in a raging wind that whipped through the village, bringing snow that created huge drifts. The path to their cabin disappeared, and snow blew in under the door. One window was a white blank—snow had drifted deep against it.

Steve stepped outside to check on the dogs and gasped as numbing cold sucked the air from his lungs. Snow was blowing against him in horizontal gusts, driven by wind that cut through his fur parka as if it were made out of a sheet.

The dogs were invisible, mere humps beside the cabin, and he knew better than to disturb them. He brought in three huge armloads of wood and went back to bed.

The next day was Sunday, but there would be no church. The blizzard had finally moved on, leaving the village utterly quiet, exhausted. No one was splitting wood. No dogs howled. Smoke rose from the larger drifts that had buried entire cabins.

Liz fried caribou steaks with their breakfast pancakes, and Steve began the long job of shoveling out. It would take all day.

By Monday afternoon they had tramped the airstrip smooth enough for the mail plane to land, and Steve helped Jackson carry the mail and other supplies up to the Trading Post.

After everything was safely in the storeroom, Jackson asked him about the trip to Mierow Lake. They drank coffee beside the stove in Gus's apartment, and Steve gave him a short account of what had happened. "Good thing you got back before that storm," Jackson said. "You going to be around tomorrow?"

"Sure."

Jackson smiled so broadly that his mustache quivered. "Guess I'll be down to see you then, if the weather holds. Got a couple of surprises for you."

"But tomorrow is Tuesday. The mail doesn't usually—"

"That's the first surprise."

10 Sugar Dog

The next day around noon, Steve heard a buzzing in the sky that pulled him outside. A small single-engine plane flew low over the village and dipped its wings.

"That's not the mail plane!" exclaimed Liz.

Steve shaded his eyes with one hand to get a better look. "No, that's a Piper Cub. It must be Jackson's surprise." He hurried to lace up his boots.

Charlie got down to the airstrip before him, but Steve arrived in time to watch the small yellow airplane line up with the runway and make a smooth landing. A minute later, Jackson climbed out, grinning broadly.

Steve grinned back at him. "Well, hey! Looks like one of those new Super Cubs! Is it yours?"

"Sure 'nuff. Had a chance to buy it from a friend of mine and jumped on it."

With Charlie following his every move, Steve took a look inside the cockpit, then walked around the plane, admiring it. "A fabric fuselage, like the Taylorcraft, huh?"

"Right. Lots easier to repair than metal. Not that I plan to run into anything."

It seemed that half the village had come down to examine the bright little plane.

"Oh boy, I'm in for it now," Jackson said. "They'll all want rides." But he didn't look as if he minded very much.

He smiled at the crowd and shook his head. "Too small," he said. "Steve says I should take it back."

The few Eskimos who understood English laughed good-naturedly.

Charlie pointed to the picture of a dog's head that was painted on the airplane's tail. "How come you got a dog there?"

"That's my airplane's name."

Charlie wrinkled his nose. "Dog plane?"

Jackson laughed his big booming laugh. "See the numbers on the wing? Can you read them to me?"

"It say: N-6-2-5-S-D."

"That's called a registration number. Sort of like the airplane's name." Jackson gave the broad yellow wing an affectionate tap. "When a pilot talks on the radio, he says the number of his plane, and for the letters he uses words so everyone can understand him better. I say, 'This is 625 Sugar Dog.'"

"Okay! So your plane is Sugar Dog." Charlie nodded vigorously. "Good! Very good!"

Gradually the crowd dispersed, and then Jackson turned to Steve. "Let's go up to your cabin. The second surprise is for you and Liz."

Steve looked at him curiously. He didn't seem to be carrying anything.

Jackson made them sit down at the table. "First I have to give a little speech. I don't entirely understand your work here, but I think you're doing a good thing for these people. I heard that these were available up north, and I thought you might be interested in seeing a couple. If you can't use them, that's okay by me."

From inside his jacket he took a brown paper package tied with string. He handed it to Liz. She pulled off the string, and a dozen thin black booklets spilled out onto the table. She picked one up and stared at the cover. "It's in Eskimo. *Markim Igatlga.*"

Steve leaned close as she paged through the booklet. "There's—*Jesus* and *Johnak* and *Jamesak!* It's—it's—Steve, it's a Gospel of Mark in Eskimo!"

She gave Jackson a wide-eyed smile, and he grinned at them.

Steve picked up one of the booklets and held it tightly. The Gospel of Mark in Eskimo? He hadn't even thought to pray for such a thing. "Hey." He shook his head. "I don't know what to say, Jackson. I can't tell you what . . . These are going to be . . ."

"Wonderful!" Liz exclaimed. "It's a wonderful gift! How did you ever find them?"

The pilot shrugged. "I guess there's a missionary up there, way up by Barrow, who's been working on an Eskimo New Testament. I know a guy who knows him, and he got these for me."

He flipped one of the booklets open. "I wasn't sure that it's the same kind of Eskimo they talk around here. *Yupik,* I think. Is that right?"

"*Yupik* is right," said Steve. He stared at the long, complicated-looking words filling each page. "And someday I'm going to be able to read it too."

Liz was still smiling. "Wow! When you do surprises, you really go overboard! These books! And your airplane!"

Jackson leaned back in his chair with a happy sigh. "*My* airplane. Not theirs—mine! Doesn't that have a fine ring to it?"

"It sure does," said Liz. She glanced back at the booklets. "And you'll stay for supper, won't you?"

"Wish I could! But I've got to get my Sugar Dog home before dark."

After Jackson left, Steve and Liz sat down and prayed over the little Eskimo Gospels. "Thank you, Lord, for this wonderful gift," said Steve. "I know You love these people, even more than we do. And now You've given them Your Word in their own language. Use it in a mighty way!"

The first person Steve gave a Gospel to was Tignak. The old Eskimo turned the booklet over in his hands without any change in expression. "Ah, this will be interesting. I didn't know a translation had been done." He smiled at Steve. "It will make a good textbook for you, I'd think."

Steve hadn't thought of that. "Sure." Tignak didn't seem to be as thrilled with the Gospel as they were, but of course, to him it was just another book.

In the days that followed, their language lessons seemed more practical, now that they were working in the Gospel of Mark. Tignak suggested that Steve and Liz come to his cabin for their evening study time, because the grandmother liked to hear them talk. Sarah listened silently to their discussions, and Charlie did too, when he was there.

At home, before they left for each study session, Steve and Liz prayed specifically for God to speak to Tignak through His Word. They often prayed for Victor too, and Steve wished that his friend could be in on the study sessions.

Steve didn't see anything of Victor that week, and on Saturday he asked Gus whether the young Eskimo was away on another trip.

"Yes, he's gone for a couple of weeks, trapping," said Gus. "Most of the men around here hunt for seal or walrus, just enough for the family's needs. But Victor knows that fur pelts are what bring in the dollars, and that boy is after dollars. The other day he ordered a rocking chair from the catalog, just like the one Elsa Danner has."

"He's fascinated by anything from the States," said Steve. "He and Nida used to ask us all kinds of questions."

"Well, hello, Ben Tignak," said Gus. He winked at Steve. "Now talk about a big spender! This man is my best customer."

Tignak groaned. "Comes from having a pair of kids who are learning how the rest of the world lives. I've heard about nothing but Japan since you did that study unit, Gus. Now Sarah wants more books about Japan, and Charlie's going to build a kite."

After paying for his package, Tignak took Steve's arm. "Come away from that man before he tries to sell you a refrigerator."

Steve grinned at Gus. "You know, I was just thinking about a nice Frigidaire, with a freezer compartment, to put in the back yard . . ." He waved at Gus, and he and Tignak walked out of the store together.

"I heard that Victor's out of town," Tignak said.

"That's what Gus told me."

"Would you mind having the church service at my place tomorrow?"

"Mind? Not a bit!" In his surprise, Steve almost missed the last step on the Trading Post's porch. "In fact, Victor's been wanting us to find a new place, and we've been praying about where to meet."

"Have you? Hmm." The old Eskimo's eyes sparkled. "Are you going to tell them about the Gospels of Mark?"

"Yes," said Steve. "Would you like to introduce them?"

"Exactly. And would you mind if I say a few words of my own?"

Tignak had an unusual glow about him today, Steve thought. What was he up to? "Sure, that'll be fine. I get tired of hearing myself talk."

On Sunday morning, Steve was glad to see two new families gathered in Tignak's front room. Perhaps they had come out of curiosity, but he would make sure they heard something worthwhile before they left.

After an opening prayer, they sang two songs together— one in English, and "Heavenly Sunlight" in Eskimo, the way the grandmother had taught them. Then Steve nodded to Tignak and he stood up.

Tignak spoke in Eskimo, but slowly and clearly, as if he wanted Steve to understand his words. He held up one of the black booklets. "I have been reading this book. It is written in Eskimo."

A stir of interest went through the small group.

"This book tells about God, who made the tundra and the sea and all the people. He hates evil, but He loves all the people. This tells about Jesus, the Son of God. God sent Jesus to live with the people and He did mighty works—more powerful than any shaman—to show that He came from God. But the people were evil. They killed Jesus."

Tignak's audience exclaimed in dismay.

He smiled. "Did this surprise God? No, it did not. God had planned that His perfect, holy Son would take the punishment for all the evil things people did. That punishment was death. But Jesus did not stay dead. God made Him live again."

Tignak lifted the black booklet for emphasis, and every eye watched it rise. "God says in this book that if a man will agree that he has done evil things and believe that Jesus has taken the punishment in his place, that man will belong to God. He will live with God forever."

Tignak gestured toward Steve. "When this white man came, I liked him even though he was a *cheechako.* I worked with him, changing his English words into Eskimo when he talked to you. He has told you these things I just said. I heard him, but his words slid away like the water slides off the back of a seal."

Tignak opened the Gospel of Mark to chapter four, verse thirty-seven. "Then I began to read in Eskimo, and the words stayed in my heart. Listen to what happened when Jesus Christ was in a boat with his friends.

"Toidlo tshayúkartok angiakdlo
ikōraluko imangiléralukodlo.

"All of us know what it is like to be out in a boat and caught by a storm. But Jesus stayed asleep in the boat. His friends were afraid.

"Itledlo angiam kinguane kawartok
akētínkglune. Toi tupangtsharat
kanerutlukodlo, 'Ayokutsertorta
tshatikinritan-ka akatshakātautserput?'

"And what did Jesus do?

"Toi maktok anokadlo inarkora kaneralunedlo
meramun, 'Nipaunak tlerartínrilo.' Toi
anokairtok kōnekapiglunedlo.

"When I read that he did this amazing thing, my heart was tossed and turned like the waves in a stormy ocean. Many times I have been afraid, and I was afraid again. I knew that I was an evil man."

Tignak stopped and looked around. "Yes, an evil man. I knew that only God could take away my sins. I thought about the mighty Jesus who commands the winds and the waves. I thanked Him for taking the punishment for my evil doings, and I told Him that I wanted to belong to Him." Tignak smiled. "Then there was peace in my heart, like the ocean when there is not a wave upon it."

Tignak paused, and Steve found that he had been holding his breath. He looked at Liz, saw the tears glistening in her eyes, and reached over to take her hand.

Tignak gazed across the group. "You have two people here to tell you about God's love, but my sister in Tagaktok has no one. Tomorrow I go to see her."

He sat down, and the Eskimos whispered among themselves. Steve rose slowly to his feet. "Let's pray." He thanked God for showing Tignak His great love and prayed for His blessing as Tignak traveled to Tagaktok. It was hard to keep his voice steady, so he did not pray for long. "Thank you, Lord, for giving us Your Word."

Afterwards, several people came up to look at the Gospels of Mark, and the few who could read Eskimo turned the pages, murmuring the words to themselves. They spoke to Tignak in Eskimo so rapid that Steve couldn't follow, but he could guess what they were saying.

When everyone had left, Steve clasped Tignak's hand in his own and looked into the dark eyes. "Thank God," he said.

Tignak's thin, intelligent face shone. "Yes, good friend, I thank God for what He has done. My sister will be amazed to hear what I have to say. She may not like it. Do pray for me."

That evening Steve presented him with one of the red, hardbacked Bibles, and Tignak accepted it as gratefully as if it were a rare volume bound in leather.

Tignak left the next morning for Tagaktok, and Steve missed him all week. There wasn't anything he could do for Tignak's family, since Charlie was quite capable of caring for them. Liz and Sarah continued to work together with the Story Club, and Liz took several meals over and stayed to visit with the grandmother.

On Thursday, Steve had planned to take a two-day hunting trip up the river with Henry, a cousin of Victor's, but in the morning Henry squinted at the sky and said, "Bad storm coming."

He glanced at Steve with his serious brown eyes. "No go." Steve knew better than to argue with him. He waved his thanks and went back to the cabin.

"Someday I'll get used to this weather," he muttered to himself. He split plenty of wood and made sure the water barrel was full, then sat down and wrote letters for the rest of the morning.

In the late afternoon, a shuffle of feet told him that someone was at the door. Liz opened it. "Come in, Sarah," she exclaimed. "What's the matter, honey?"

The girl's round face had lost its brightness, and her eyes were huge with worry. "Charlie. He gone. He tell me not to say anything, but he not come back."

She looked at Steve and her lower lip trembled. "He take Mikki."

11 Am-nok Again

Steve grabbed for his parka. Outside, the temperature had dropped, and a wind blew off the tundra, lifting dry snow from the ground, flinging it in his face.

Henry had said a storm was coming.

Yes, Mikki was gone, and so was Bigfoot. Tignak had taken his dog team and the big sled to Tagatok, so all Charlie had was the small sled and Steve's two dogs. The tracks in the snow angled off from the cabin to the east, toward the Tiskleet River.

He ran back into the cabin. Liz had an arm around Sarah and was talking softly. Steve stood over them, his heart hammering with impatience. "Sarah, think very carefully. Did Charlie say anything about where he was going?"

She started to shake her head, then stopped. "Yesterday he say something about Shanaluk."

Gently Liz asked, "Did he have any friends in Shanaluk that he might go to visit?"

"No." Sarah frowned. "He not have so many friends. Sometime he go to Joseph cabin when Am-nok there."

Steve's jaw tightened. He'd gone to Am-nok.

"When did he leave?"

"After lunch time. First he go to school." Sarah's voice shook. "I tell him bad storm, but he don't care."

"I'm going after him," said Steve. "He'll never get to Shanaluk before this storm hits. And the tundra will be . . . Pray that he kept to the river."

Liz stood up, looking anxious. "Don't you think—"

"Pack me some food," said Steve. "And a thermos of strong tea with plenty of sugar. Food for the dogs. An extra parka. One of those blankets. Overnight stuff. The tent . . ."

Liz stared at him, then turned away to fill the kettle with water.

He caught up an armful of gear and hurried outside. Better not take too much, with only three dogs.

Patch would have to lead. Maybe Howler and Bandit could keep from fighting long enough to work together. Should he try to borrow more dogs? Tignak was gone. Victor was gone. No. No time.

His hands shook as he harnessed the dogs and pulled a rope tightly across the load. Liz had turned white, but when he hugged her good-bye, all she said was, "We'll be praying."

The dogs were not especially eager to run, but they bent into the harness and he shouted encouragement to his new leader. "*Gih,* Patch! You can do it, boy!" The black and white dog had only one eye, but he was strong and smart.

Light snow began to powder the sled as he reached the river, and by the time an hour had passed, it fell so thickly he could hardly see past the dogs' bushy tails. The wind blew as if it were sweeping through a tunnel, sending snow into his face, along with ice crystals that cut like tiny razors.

At a bend in the river, Patch faltered, and the dogs behind him slowed. What was the matter with him? Steve couldn't see anything in the whirling snow.

He felt his way up the towline, talking to the dogs. "You guys can do this. I know you can." He took Patch's head in his hands to talk to him, and saw that the eyelid on his good eye was frozen shut. No wonder he hadn't made the turn. The dog was running blind.

Gently he warmed the dog's face with his bare hands, and a minute later the brown eye opened. Patch shook his head back and forth and whined. Hoping that meant he was okay for now, Steve pulled his mittens back over his stiffening hands. The other two dogs seemed okay.

"*Gih!* Patch!" They started off again, and Steve ran beside the sled to get warm, bending low to keep his face out of the icy wind.

The light was fading fast, and there would be no moon. Where was Charlie by now? He tried to calculate the time that had passed. The boy might still be on the river trail. Surely he wouldn't have turned off to cross the tundra at the usual place. But he couldn't have stopped for the night, not without some shelter.

Maybe he was counting on Mikki to know the way. Even in the dark? Or maybe he had turned back, and Steve would meet up with him, just ahead.

Hope rose, warming him for the next few miles, but finally he had to admit that it wasn't going to happen. And the dogs were growing tired from running against this headwind.

He peered through the snow and tried to make sense of his frantic thoughts. Better stop for the night while he still had a choice. He slowed the dogs to a halt.

Working blind, stumbling with exhaustion and worry, he took a long time to get a twig fire going and unharness the dogs. He threw them generous portions of dried salmon, gave them some snow water, and let them burrow into a snow drift. They would be okay.

Then, battling the wind, he tramped down a space beside the willows and finally got his tent set up. Too tired to cook, he chewed up some dried caribou, drank snow water, and crawled into his sleeping bag.

There was no way to get warm, really warm, but at least he was out of the wind. He fell into an exhausted sleep and minutes later jerked awake. How could Charlie survive in this? How far had he gone?

Panic beat in his chest. If something happened to that boy . . . No, it couldn't. Yes, it could. And how would he explain it to Tignak?

He drowsed and woke again to the nightmare that would not go away. Snow whispered against the tent, and he listened to it for a long time, curled into a shivering ball. Again he drowsed and woke with a start. *Am-nok.* Why would the boy rush off to see him? Just thinking about the shaman made him clench his hands.

Hadn't Charlie heard enough of the truth to know that Am-nok had no real answers? And why did the boy listen to Elsa Danner? Because of her nonsense, he had risked his life to shoot a seal, and he actually believed that she could make him an amulet!

"You hate her," Charlie had said. Maybe so. Why couldn't she leave him alone?

If only Charlie would listen to God's Word—but perhaps it hadn't been properly explained. Somehow, he had failed the boy.

It was too cold to sleep any more. He turned on the flashlight to look at his watch. It would be dawn in an hour or so. Stiffly he crawled out of the tent and gathered branches for a fire. The wind had dropped, but snow still fell, dry and fine.

The dogs awoke only when he nudged them, and he had to drag them out of their burrows. He gave them some water and drank a quick bowl of soup himself. He harnessed the dogs, fumbling at the stiff leather with urgent fingers. If Charlie had survived the night, even an hour's difference could determine whether he lived through this day.

They started off into the icy gray dawn, and as they raced up the frozen river he tried to watch both banks at once. The snow would have covered any tracks, but he couldn't help looking.

A man and his son had frozen to death out on the pack ice this winter in Koyalik. The memory blew through his mind, so cold, so daunting that he almost missed the turnoff for Shanaluk.

The marker, a pair of old, twisted trees on the river bank, was drifted deep in snow, and he had to help the dogs by pushing the sled through the drifts, up onto the tundra.

They set off once more, the snow falling less and less, the sky growing lighter. But the cold! It crept through all his layers of fur and wool and ached in his hands and feet. He hunched his shoulders and swung his arms to keep warm.

Endless white. Endless silence. He tried to shout to the dogs, but his voice came out as a croak.

He tried again.

"*Gih,* Patch! *Gih,* Howler! *Gih,* Bandit! Got to find Charlie. And Mikki and Bigfoot. They're your pals."

He shouted to the scrawny willows at the river, to the frozen white wilderness, to the pale streak of light in the east. He shouted to keep up his courage and to hear the sound of a human voice.

Then from somewhere came an answering cry. A wolf's howl, wild and despairing.

Or was it? He turned the dogs toward the sound. He shouted to the white horizon.

He heard it again.

He squinted across the snowfield. Was that a black speck? Or was his mind playing tricks on him?

"*Gih,* Patch, *gih!*" If only he had a whip! But the dogs were running as fast as they could.

He jumped off the sled to lighten their load, taking long, swift steps in his snowshoes.

The black speck was a dog. Beside it was an overturned sled. Steve's heart caught in his throat. Don't think. Just run. Get there in time.

Mikki was crouched over something beneath the sled. He looked up at Steve and whined.

A bundle of furs, drifted with snow.

Charlie.

Steve put an arm under the boy and brushed away the snow. He bent close, and his panting breaths stirred the straggling dark hair on the boy's forehead. Was he? . . . Yes, he was alive.

A hump of fur beside Charlie stirred and sat up. Bigfoot. So that was how Charlie had survived the night. He had slept under the sled, between the two dogs.

He gathered the boy into his arms. "Thank you, Lord."

Mikki whined again, sitting back on his haunches, looking expectant. "Good dog! Good dogs, both of you," said Steve. "Gonna feed you soon."

He shook the rest of the snow off Charlie and carried him to the sled. The boy's hands dangled uselessly. Steve took one look at them and jerked open his parka and shirt. He placed the frozen hands against his bare stomach and pulled the warm clothing back over them. He held Charlie close, rubbing his arms and legs until the boy began to groan and writhe with pain.

"It sure does hurt, doesn't it?" Steve remembered his own experience with frostbite. "But that's a good sign."

As soon as Charlie's hands had thawed, he pulled off the boy's mukluks and rubbed his feet. They were white and cold, but the tissue under the skin was still soft; they'd be okay.

By now, Charlie was struggling to sit up, so he wrapped him in the extra parka and the blanket and helped him drink tea from the thermos. The boy's face was pale and blank, and he did not seem to recognize Steve.

Got to get him out of this cold.

Steve lashed him onto the sled, fed Mikki and Bigfoot, and harnessed them into the team. Then, towing Tignak's small sled behind them, he turned the dogs toward Koyalik. Mikki pulled at top speed, as if he understood Steve's urgency, and the tired dogs followed his lead.

They made record time down the river trail, but even so, by the time they reached Koyalik, Charlie had lapsed again into unconsciousness. If only there were a doctor in the village, or even a nurse!

Liz greeted him with a pale smile as he carried the boy into the cabin, then turned her attention to Charlie. "Let's get him into something dry and warm."

They put him on the big bunk, and Steve helped her strip off the boy's icy clothes.

"What's this?" she asked.

Steve lifted the dirty leather string that Charlie wore around his neck. "His owl claws," he said. "To give him good hunting. Poor kid."

They rubbed his arms and legs some more, checked his feet and hands, dressed him in some of Steve's clothes, and rolled him in their thickest wool blanket.

By the time they finished, the color was returning to Charlie's face and he opened his eyes. He sat up to drink some tea and then a cup of thick soup. He gazed around the cabin without saying anything, and he would not look at Steve or Liz.

Liz put a hand on the boy's shoulder. "I'm going to find Sarah," she said. "Back in a while. Get strong, Charlie."

The boy didn't answer, and after she'd gone, silence grew heavy in the cabin.

Steve couldn't stand it any longer. He sat down on the edge of the bunk. "Hey, what's the matter, kid? I don't usually bite on Fridays. Won't even talk to me?"

Charlie looked up at him with eyes that brimmed with misery. "I very so sorry. I steal your dogs and make lotsa trouble for you."

For a minute, Steve could not speak. Then he said, "I'm not angry, Charlie. But why did you do it?"

The boy shifted. "I go to Shanaluk."

"Why?"

Charlie flexed his hands, wincing at the pain. He picked up a corner of the blanket and let it drop. "I get seal for Mrs. Danner, but she not make seal claws to hang on my parka. So I go talk to Am-nok. I want to ask for amulet. Maybe he give me walrus teeth, so when I go on ice, I not scared."

Steve picked up Charlie's hand and held it. Strong brown fingers. Clever fingers that could build a trap or set a snare or skin a rabbit in minutes. He curled his own fingers around the boy's hand. "I have been scared lots of times, Charlie."

"Then what do you do?"

"I talk to God."

The boy shook his head and gently pulled his hand away. He hunched down into the blankets, rolled to face the wall, and closed his eyes.

His breathing soon leveled into sleep, and the cabin was so quiet that Steve could hear the clock ticking.

He stayed where he was, remembering his worry, his desperate fear last night. And his anger at Am-nok and the Danner woman.

Fear. Hatred.

"I talk to God," he'd told Charlie. But today, in the midst of his own fear, he'd forgotten about God. Again.

He fell to his knees beside the bed. After a time, he whispered, "Father, I have sinned. Take away this hatred for my enemies and replace it with Thy love. And I have forgotten You and the promise You gave me. I am afraid. I am so afraid for Charlie."

He spread out both hands, palms upward, on the blanket. "Here is Charlie. Here is this ministry. They are yours. Let me *not* be dismayed. Give me courage to trust what You are doing."

The sound of voices outside the cabin brought him slowly to his feet. He glanced at Charlie. The boy's eyes opened, blinked, and opened again. By the time Liz and Sarah came through the door, Steve was there to meet them.

"Liz," he said, "I think this young man is ready for some real food. Where's the rest of that roast we had?"

Tignak returned the next day, and by then Charlie had regained his strength and was doing his usual chores. Steve decided to let the boy tell his father what had happened.

That evening, Tignak stopped by after supper and reported that his sister had been glad to see him. He wanted to go back soon. The lines on his face seemed more deeply carved tonight, and Steve knew he was worried about Charlie.

After they had talked for a while, Tignak stood up and put on his parka. Before he opened the door, he looked at Steve. "I owe you much, my friend. First, for introducing me to Jesus Christ. And now, for saving my son's life. I apologize on his behalf and ask you to pray with me that God will change his heart."

Steve clasped Tignak's outstretched hand. "Yes. It will be God's work. I am trying to learn that."

On the following Thursday, Jackson stopped by for a quick visit, and after he'd eaten a handful of cookies, he asked whether Steve had found the Gospels of Mark useful.

"I sure have," Steve said. "Gave one to Ben Tignak right away." He described the impact it had made on Tignak.

"Well now, that's a puzzle," said Jackson. "He's the best educated Eskimo I've met, that Tignak. He has read the Bible before, hasn't he?"

Steve poured more coffee for them both. "Yes, and he could quote verses from it just like he can quote sonnets from Shakespeare. But there's nothing like reading something in your own language. Those words speak to the heart. I think God helped Tignak understand what he was reading, probably for the first time."

"Well, I'm sure glad you could use those things."

Steve smiled. "Problem is, I'm greedy. I'd like to buy a bunch of them—enough to give to anybody who wants one. I'd love to take them to that village up by Mierow Lake."

"They're not very expensive," said Jackson. "When are you going back to Mierow Lake?"

"Not for a while, I guess. It takes three days by dog sled to get there."

"Hey!" Jackson put down his mug with a thump. "Want me to fly you up there in the Cub? An old friend of mine lives sort of near there, in Huslia. And I've got a week of vacation coming."

"Great!" exclaimed Steve. "At least let me pay for the gas."

"It's a deal." Jackson grinned. "Just say when."

12 Searching the Ice

"It's a good thing we didn't try to fly into Mierow Lake this week," Steve said to Liz. He dumped his armload of wood into the box beside the stove. "Seems like we've had one storm after another."

As he took off his parka, he glanced at the window, but he couldn't see anything for the spreading patches of frost. "Feels like another one's on its way."

She smiled at him. "Maybe it's a good afternoon to get some serious work done on those verses in Mark, the ones Tignak gave us. Then when he comes over tonight, he'll be pleased—"

Voices outside the door interrupted her. Henry and Victor's uncle stood on the doorstep, hunched against the wind. Henry peered at Steve past the deep ruff on his parka. "The white woman. She go out on the ice." His brown eyes were worried. "We look for her. Can you come with dogs?"

"Sure."

Steve put on extra clothes under his caribou furs and parka, harnessed the dogs, and joined the group of men and dog teams gathered outside the Trading Post. The sun was lost in a bank of somber clouds, and wind blew off the ice with a hard, metallic chill. He had to lean close to hear the leader's instructions.

The rescue operation seemed extremely well organized, but rescue teams often went out onto the ice, so perhaps it was like a volunteer fire department in which everyone knew what to do.

He and Victor's uncle were sent to search the area off shore from the southern edge of the village, and he was content to let the older man lead the way. For the first half-mile, the ice was covered with snow packed as hard as wood by the pounding winds, almost flat except for a few low hummocks.

They soon reached the first ridges. Polar ice floes, driven down through the Bering Strait by north winds, had struck the shore ice and become great mounds and spires of ice mixed with sand and rock. These *eewoonucks* formed an icy wilderness between the shelf ice at the shore and the frozen sea, the pack ice. Steve stared at the tumbled slabs, clear green and blue, some four feet thick. It would be easy to get lost out here. And terrifying.

Victor's uncle left his dogs at the foot of a towering ridge and, although he was stooped and old, climbed it with quick strides. Steve followed more slowly.

Together they scanned the vast expanse of jagged ice. Victor's uncle muttered, "The ice like a mean dog. He wait for you to stop watching, then he try to get you." He shook his head. "We go more south." They scrambled back down to the waiting dogs.

For hours, it seemed, they twisted between ridges and around hummocks, and the wind blew more and more strongly. It moaned among the eewoonucks and sent snow swirling into Steve's face. His legs and feet had been cold for a long time, and now, in spite of the fur ruff on his parka, cold needled his cheek bones, turning his face numb.

What must Elsa Danner be thinking as she wandered through this, alone? What if she should die out here . . . and have to face the anger of a holy God, without Christ? For the first time, he felt a stirring of pity for the woman. "Thank you, Lord, for changing my heart," he whispered. And he began to pray that God would mercifully allow her to be found.

Snow fell more thickly and Victor's uncle turned his team toward shore. The dogs picked up their pace and soon they reached the village with its welcoming lights.

A man hurrying back from the Trading Post stopped to give them news. "They find white woman. Take her to her house. She okay."

That evening they talked with Tignak about the rescue. "She was glad to see us, I think." Tignak's eyes gleamed. "Her manner was—shall we say—somewhat less frosty than usual. She was babbling something about talking to the spirits, but no one took her seriously. People who are lost on the ice come back saying strange things."

Had she claimed to be speaking to the Spirit of the Sea? Liz sent Steve a glance. She must be remembering Elsa Danner's comments about superstitious Eskimos.

Tignak was opening their books on the table for another study session.

"She often walks out on the ice by herself, doesn't she?" asked Liz.

"Yes, but she shouldn't," said Tignak. "And I have warned her. Perhaps she will not do it any more."

Steve sighed. "A strange, angry person. A needy person," he said. "Is Charlie still doing jobs for her?"

"She keeps him busy after school. Today she had him shoot two dozen ptarmigan." Tignak picked up a notebook. "Odd. I can't imagine why she would want so many, but she pays him well. Too well."

His leathery fingers tightened on the notebook. "My son is learning what money can buy. He saw a knife at the Trading Post and he's saving every penny he gets."

"You do not like this?" asked Liz, her voice gentle.

In his agitation, Tignak's English became less polished. "I do not like money to be important to him. And there is a bad spirit in that woman. I do not like Charlie to be with her so much. I pray for him."

The old man's face creased with pain, and Liz changed the subject. They spent the rest of the evening practicing Eskimo words, and Steve had more trouble than ever keeping the endings straight.

Charlie . . . Elsa Danner . . . Lord, protect that boy!

By the time Jackson had made arrangements for his vacation, another week passed, but finally the details were all settled for their trip to Mierow Lake.

Jackson would fly Steve to Mierow Lake, stay overnight, spend the next two or three days visiting his friend Jake, then come back to pick him up.

"Steve, I just don't like the idea of your being alone there for three days," said Liz. "I know those people have been kind to you and most of them seem to be Christians, but . . ."

"I understand." Steve pulled their box of papers out from under the table. "But you need to stay here with your Story Club kids, and besides, there isn't room in that Cub for another person."

He found his list of trip supplies and added to it: *Extra Gospels of Mark. Ask Jackson.*

Liz stared off into a dark corner of the cabin. "How about . . . No, that won't work. Steve! How about taking

Mikki? He'd be some protection at least. If I needed a dog team, I'd ask Tignak anyway."

Steve considered. "Might work. Good thing Mikki is small. If he weighed as much as some huskies, we'd be over gross for sure. I'll ask Jackson."

The following Tuesday afternoon, 625 Sugar Dog took off from Koyalik into a sky as blue as polar ice. The little plane rolled for three hundred feet before lifting off into the cold air. Not as fast as usual, Steve thought, but we're heavily loaded.

The plane was narrow, with his seat behind Jackson's, as if they were astride the same horse. They wore headsets so they could talk over the roar of the Cub's engine.

He glanced behind him. Mikki looked fairly comfortable, curled inside the cargo net they'd hooked up to keep him from sliding around in the plane. Jackson had taken the dog up once already, just to see how he'd react to a plane ride, and he'd behaved perfectly.

"Good dog," said Steve. "And don't even think about chewing your way out. We'll be there soon." Mikki gave him an innocent stare, and Steve laughed aloud.

The Cub made a low pass over the village, and he leaned close to the window, waving. Liz and the others waved from below, growing smaller every minute.

Lord, take care of her, he prayed, wondering at the sudden apprehension he felt. But Tignak was nearby, and Charlie could probably be counted on in an emergency.

Charlie! The lurch in his stomach had nothing to do with the airplane, climbing now for altitude. But the Danner woman seemed to be acting more sensibly these days. Henry said that she didn't go out on the ice any more, although she did walk down to the shore every evening. "To talk to the seals," she had told someone.

Jackson spoke through the headset. "Recognize that?" He pointed below them to a scattering of cabins beside a thread-like river and a frozen lake that looked as big as a silver dollar.

"Shanaluk?" asked Steve.

Jackson nodded.

A whole day's trip in half an hour! And less than two hours to get to Mierow Lake. A missionary could do a lot in this country with an airplane.

It didn't seem likely that he'd have one any time soon. But they would pray some more, like Peter kept telling them to. Just this morning Liz had thanked God for the Cub and confidently asked for one of their own. He'd rather have something bigger, himself, but a Cub would certainly be better than nothing.

The country slipped past below them, a wide, white expanse of tundra dotted with frozen lakes. Steve whistled to himself, watching a small band of caribou move across the tundra. Behind the caribou trotted three wolves.

Soon they were approaching the mountains, and the Cub climbed higher. A river, its ice bare and gleaming, twisted through countless white-wrinkled ridges and folds. The trees looked like coarse fur poking up through the snow. And that must be Mierow Lake, a crescent shape, deep in a long valley and edged with trees.

Jackson circled, slowing the Cub, and floated down toward the lake. The cabins at its southern edge showed up clearly. "I'll check out the ice," he said.

Wind had swept the snow on the lake into long parallel heaps, like sand dunes. He lined up on a strip of bare ice between two heaps and flew slowly down it.

"Looks okay," Jackson said. The ice was gray-green, with a few cracks webbing the surface, not the black of treacherous thin ice.

Jackson circled and made another pass, his head pressed against the window, still studying the ice, looking for hidden obstacles that could tear up his skis.

"Let's try it." He circled once more, lined up again on the bare streak, and gently set the plane down at one end. The ice bumped past under their skis, rough, but solid.

He pulled the mixture control knob, and the engine coughed to a stop. While he was still tying an insulated cover over the plane's nose, children came running across the lake. They crowded around, chattering excitedly.

"No touch!" Jackson shouted, and they all stepped back.

Then he reached into his pocket for a handful of wrapped candies. "Good kids." He tossed the candy to them, one by one, still looking stern. "Good kids get candy."

They all nodded and smiled back.

"Hey, mister," said one of the bigger boys, "I make sure no one touch your airplane."

Jackson threw him a chocolate bar and grinned at Steve. "Smart kids too."

A low whine came from the rear of the plane. "Okay, boy, I'm coming!" Steve unhooked Mikki's net. He let him step over the back seat and jump down onto the ice.

The children clapped with delight. "Lookit, wolf!" they cried. But they didn't rush up to pet Mikki, he noticed. They probably knew enough about huskies to wait and see.

They tied down the airplane as close to the shoreline as they could, and Jackson seemed relieved that Steve's cabin was right at the edge of the lake. They chained Mikki near the cabin.

"Keep an eye on my Sugar Dog," Jackson said, and the husky thumped his tail in reply.

By the time they had swept out the cabin and unpacked their supplies, the sun was setting, and Jackson decided to stay for the night.

Steve went looking for Samson or Jacob Nanouk. Samson was away on a hunting trip, but Nanouk was there and his cabin was filled with men.

Nanouk waved a plump hand at him and continued talking to the men. They seemed to be discussing plans for a new building.

Steve waited until the discussion was over, then he showed Nanouk a Gospel of Mark and asked about having meetings during the next few days.

Nanouk looked doubtful. "Okay for women, maybe. But men very busy. We build a new store. Big enough for everything."

He gestured to show that it would be very big indeed, then looked at the black booklet Steve had given him. "Good," he said. "I read this sometime. Thank you. Maybe we talk sometime before you go back."

Steve smiled in spite of his disappointment. "Sure. I'll be here. Any time." He stopped to visit in a few cabins on the way back to his own. Samson wasn't expected back for a few days, and no one wanted to talk about anything except the new building.

A pile of trimmed spruce logs stood near the lake. It looked as if they'd already started on their project.

At his cabin door, he paused to knock the snow off his mukluks. So why had the Lord brought him all the way over here at this particular time?

He went inside to start frying the caribou steaks Liz had sent along. Jackson had already started a fire in the wood stove. "Make some plans?" he asked.

"No plans," Steve said. "And Nanouk didn't seem all that thrilled with the Gospel of Mark." He had planned to preach from the fourth chapter of Mark, the story of Christ calming the storm—if he got a chance.

Fat sizzled in the skillet, reminding him of what he was supposed to be doing. He dropped the red slabs of meat into the pan, but for once the aroma of frying steaks didn't lift his spirits.

He and Jackson sat up late that night. Jackson talked about flying Wildcats during the war, but part of Steve's mind was busy wondering what he should do tomorrow. Help them build their store?

Finally Jackson yawned, saying he wanted to get an early start tomorrow, and they turned off the lantern. The fire had burned low, and chilly air crept in under the door and around the window frame. Moonlight glimmered through the snow-flecked, grimy window, and Steve thought sleepily about getting up to see how the frozen lake looked under the moon. Then he could tell Liz . . .

An explosion of snarls and growls came from outside.

Mikki?

He yanked on his mukluks and parka, and snatched up his rifle. Jackson was banging around in the dark, yelling something about the Cub. Steve found the door and burst through it with Jackson at his heels.

13 Taboos

Mikki, a furious dark blur, leaped at the end of his chain. Moonlight lay across the frozen lake and glinted off the airplane, which rocked back and forth on its skis.

Something was attacking it from the lake side, the side they couldn't see.

Steve spoke to Mikki and he quieted, growling deep in his throat.

Jackson was beside him now, rifle in hand. "Get downwind," he whispered. Together they ran from shadow to shadow along the shore until they could see around the plane.

A tall dark shape took a swipe at the side of the plane, back where they'd carried their gear. The wind blew lightly toward them, bringing a smell like sweaty socks.

Bear.

The hairs on Steve's neck prickled. The bear shook its head back and forth and clicked its teeth with a sound that rang through the air. Steve lifted his rifle, chambered a round, and heard Jackson do the same.

Steve's bullet hit the bear's neck. Jackson's shot went low, into its back.

It turned toward them, hopping stiff-legged and growling.

Steve chambered another round; this shot hit the bear's shoulder. It staggered, and Jackson's bullet took it to the ground.

He reloaded fast, but the bear lay still.

Slowly they walked across to the great mound of fur on the ice.

"A big old rascal," said Jackson.

"Don't the bears around here hibernate?"

"Sure, but it's April already." Jackson stooped and lightly touched the long brown fur. "This old guy woke up early, I guess. Did you see the way he charged us instead of running off? Plenty ornery!"

He unlocked the airplane to get a flashlight, and together they checked the damage to the Cub. The bear had torn a ragged hole in the side of the plane's fuselage. Shreds of fabric lay on the ice. "Whew!" said Jackson. "I've heard of this happening, but I never thought I'd see it."

"What was he after?" asked Steve.

"Maybe smelled the dog. Or the dried salmon I had in there yesterday. Some pilots keep a bag of mothballs around. I should've brought some."

Their gunshots must have awakened the whole village. A dozen Eskimo men had appeared; they stood in a circle around the dead bear. Steve wondered at their silence, but just now he didn't want to ask the reason.

He shifted his rifle from one hand to the other. "Well," he said to Jackson, "are we going to skin it now or wait until morning?"

Jackson touched Steve's arm and took him back to the tail of the airplane, as if to show him something. "Careful," he said in a low voice. "This is a brown bear. They've got all kinds of taboos about brown bears. We might be smart to give it to them—as a gift, you know—and let them handle it the way they want to."

Steve had recognized some of the men in the group. "These people are supposed to be Christians."

"Never mind what they call themselves. When it comes to angering the spirits or whatever, it's the old customs that really count."

Steve shook his head tiredly. "Okay, give them the bear."

Jackson talked to one of the older men, and the whole group nodded solemnly. Mikki had started yowling, so Steve tramped back across the ice to join him.

He sat down beside the dog, pulling the furry head close. "Good boy, good boy." The dog relaxed against him. "If it weren't for you, he'd have ripped that plane apart and we'd be stuck here forever, maybe. Good dog!"

He rested his face against Mikki's neck and breathed in the warm, musky dog smell. A good smell. He closed his eyes. "There's lots of work for us to do here, Mik." The dog licked his face, leaving long wet streaks that froze immediately. Steve rubbed the ice off his face and tousled the dog's ears. He stood to his feet. "Okay, time for bed."

The Eskimos couldn't have slept much that night, because by the time Steve got up to make breakfast, the bear had been removed from the ice and the village bustled with activity.

He and Jackson ate quickly, then walked out to take a look at the Cub. Mikki raced ahead of them, and Steve called him back when he saw what had been left on the ice.

For some reason, the Eskimos had placed the bear's head at the spot where it was killed, with its nose turned toward the mountains.

Steve grabbed at Mikki's thick ruff and spoke sternly. "No! Don't touch it. Understand? Stay by me."

The dog whined, but he sat down on his haunches, sniffing the ice.

Jackson studied the hole in the plane's fabric, then rummaged through his survival gear and came up with a piece of canvas, an oversized needle, and heavy thread. "I've seen worse," he said. "This won't be too bad." He threaded the needle as if he'd been sewing all his life. "At least the bear didn't get my wings and tail. Thanks to ol' Mikki."

The dog looked up at the sound of his name and rose to his feet, looking eager. "No," said Steve. "Down. Don't you move a hair."

He held the ragged strips of fabric in place while Jackson stitched them loosely together. Then Jackson cut a large patch out of the canvas and began to sew it over the hole with small, tight stitches.

"That's all you have to do, huh?" asked Steve.

"Just want to keep the air from getting inside the plane and slowing it down. This will work until I get back to Nome."

"Well, I'd better take Mikki away from this big temptation," said Steve. "And I want to find out what's happening in the village."

He chained Mikki beside the cabin and went to find Jacob Nanouk. The man was sitting by the stove in the small general store, sharpening his knife. After the usual talk about the weather, Steve ventured to say, "The bear's head. It was left on the ice?"

Nanouk gave him a quick glance, then looked away. "Yes. So the soul of the bear will return to the mountains and take flesh as a new bear."

Steve nodded, remembering that Eskimos thought each animal had a soul. "What will you do with the bear?" he asked.

"We treat bear with respect so its soul will not be angry. So village will not starve. We have ceremony. Make presents and bring them to the bear. Women and children must not eat the meat."

Nanouk bent over his knife as if the subject was closed, and Steve left quietly.

Again the question came. Why had God brought him here *now?* These people were so wrapped up in their ceremonies and their building program that they obviously didn't want to listen to him.

By mid-afternoon, Jackson had finished patching the Cub, and Steve thought he had done a good job. "Serviceable," said the pilot. He stowed his gear back in the plane. "I've got to get going, but first, let's eat." He gave Steve a mischievous grin. "I'm hungry enough to eat a bear."

"Careful!" Steve told him what he'd learned, and Jackson gave him a sympathetic glance. "Want to come on to Huslia with me? Jake would love to meet you."

Steve tried to smile. "Thanks, but I think not. For some reason, God wants me here."

He and Mikki went out to see Jackson off, and after the little plane had disappeared over the mountains, Steve wished he had accepted Jackson's offer. Sounds of merriment came from the village, reminding him of what was going on there. Plenty of feasting and dancing, no doubt. And it would go on all night.

"Let's go for a walk, Mik." He set out along the strip of bare ice that Jackson had used as a runway, and concentrated on enjoying the spruce-scented air.

At the far end of the lake he found a wide trail that led up the side of the ridge. "Let's see how far up this goes. It should be a great view."

The trail curved back and forth, climbing through the forest in easy stages, and after an hour or so, Steve discovered why it was so well used. He came to a small clearing littered with spruce branches. Half-buried stumps showed that this was where the Eskimos had been cutting down spruce trees.

The trail wound up the ridge from clearing to clearing, and after an hour of hiking, he thought they should be almost to the top. The trail ended at another clearing, but a narrow path led off to one side, climbing even higher. Someone else had wanted to find a lookout spot.

Or maybe not. A long time later he was still climbing and the path was growing fainter and fainter; he began to wonder whether he was following an animal trail. Snowshoes would have made for better walking in this soft stuff, faster than mukluks. Too bad he hadn't thought of that.

The sight of open sky beyond the trees beckoned him a little farther. He let Mikki go first, then stepped cautiously through the branches. What a view!

On every side rose the snow-covered mountains, their slopes and gullies filled with ranks of trees, gray-blue in the afternoon light. An eagle circled up toward him in ascending spirals. Below were tiny cabins drifted with snow, a wisp of gray smoke rising from each one, rising until it was lost in the pearly sky.

He stood there for a while, praying for the people of Mierow Lake, until the cold seeped into his feet and warned him to keep moving. He took a last glance. The smoky threads above the cabins were fainter now, disappearing . . .

A swirl of snowflakes suddenly erased the village, and Steve glanced at the sky in alarm. A snowstorm? This could not be happening.

He turned and ran back the way he had come, taking great leaping strides, dodging around the turns in the path, until he was gasping for breath. But there was no time to rest. This path was the only way to get back and soon it would disappear under the snow.

Wind, laden with snow, whirled through the trees. His breath came hard, and a pain began somewhere in his side. He slipped, almost falling in his haste. Got to keep going. Faster.

No food. No shelter. A storm. Panic knifed through his thoughts, sharpened by the discouragement he had felt all day.

No! *Be not dismayed.*

He slowed to a purposeful walk. This time he would not forget. The Lord would show him what to do. He began to pray, asking for wisdom, for energy, for courage. Finishing, he said, "This is Your work, Lord. And I belong to You. Keep me trusting."

Even here under the trees, the snow was so thick, so wind-driven, that he couldn't see a yard in front of him. Mikki kept disappearing from sight, then reappearing, looking up at him as if to say, "Shouldn't we stop?" The dog knew better than to keep going in this.

He went a little farther, hampered by the deep snow, wondering if he had lost the path, and came to a small clearing. He stumbled into a buried stump. Was this one of the places where they had cut down trees? Yes. And there would be spruce branches here.

With new energy, he pulled at a snow-drifted pile of branches and shook them free of snow. He arranged them into a crude barrier against the wind. The smaller branches would serve for bedding. If only he had a tarp! Or even a snow knife for making some kind of a shelter.

Was there any point in trying a fire? The surrounding trees had been stripped of dead branches—the Eskimos had probably scavenged them for kindling—but after several minutes he found one small dead branch and stretched high to pull it off the tree. Huddling against his barrier, he broke the branch up into a handful of twigs, then used his pocket knife to shred the twigs so they would catch and hold a flame.

His hands shaking with cold, he lit a match and watched as it burned along its length and flared into the twigs. A tiny flame burned for a few minutes, but as soon as he added some green spruce tips, it smoked and went out. He tried again, shielding the twigs with his hands, letting the fire get hotter before he tried the green stuff. Too bad that was all he had for fuel.

While it still burned feebly, he warmed his hands and picked up a handful of snow. It melted into slush that tasted pretty good. He melted another mouthful, then carefully put a tuft of spruce needles into the flames. They sizzled for an instant and went out. He used one more of his precious matches to relight the last of the twigs, but before long they burned away and the fire was a smoking heap, sodden with falling snow.

He'd better forget the fire.

But he needed some way to stay warm.

Mikki, digging into the snow to make a burrow, gave him an idea. At least his hands were warmer now, and his fur mittens would keep them dry. He knelt in the snow and scooped it up against the barrier of branches until he had made a huge mound. The snow was too light and dry to stay in place very well, but he managed to hollow it out like the snow caves he used to make as a boy. He put down more branches for a floor, called Mikki to join him, and piled up snow to close the opening.

Mikki immediately curled into a ball and Steve curved his body around the dog, crossing his arms over his chest.

He tried to think what time it was. It had taken a long time to dig out the shelter. Maybe only five or six hours until morning. He felt himself drifting off to sleep and awoke, shivering. Mikki shifted on the branches, probably wishing he were alone in his own snow burrow. The dog's body was solid beside him, almost warm if he used his imagination.

He thought about Liz—she seemed to be on his mind a lot this trip—and prayed for her. He prayed for Charlie and Elsa Danner, for Tignak, and for the work at Koyalik.

He drowsed and woke again. Had the storm gone yet? No, the wind was still moaning through the trees.

He prayed for the ministry at Mierow Lake, asking God to make something good come out of this trip. He tried not to think about food, especially sizzling caribou steaks, fried crisp on the outside with potatoes and onions, the way Liz did them.

He licked his dry lips; they felt windburned. It would be nice to have some of that cool snow water, right about now. Should he go out and take a chance on finding another few twigs? Not likely. And he knew that it wasn't a good idea to melt snow in his mouth because it would use too much of his body's heat.

To distract himself, he talked to God about an airplane. It would make such a difference, save so much time, allow him to reach so many more people. Not a huge plane, he thought dreamily, but not as small as the Cub. Maybe big enough to carry four people and plenty of gear. Red and white? Blue with red stripes?

Cold—aching, numbing cold—seeped through his clothes. He tried to wiggle his toes and couldn't. Getting numb? Should do something about that. He put his arms around the dog and the bushy tail wagged.

Be not dismayed.

Thank you, Lord, for Mikki. For dry clothes, at least. For this place where they cut the trees . . .

Something was tugging at his parka. Cold air blew into his face. Mikki stood over him, whining.

Steve sat up with a groan and stared dizzily at an opening in his cave. Snow still fell, but dim light filtered through the trees. It must be morning. He could see to the end of the clearing.

Slowly he crawled out of the shelter and pulled himself to his feet. His feet and legs were stiff, but he staggered off in what he hoped was the right direction. Mikki trotted in front of him, his tail waving as if he'd had a fine night's sleep.

From one clearing to the next he plodded, forcing his legs to move. At least he seemed to be going downhill. His feet tingled and ached, but he reminded himself that pain was a good sign. Most important was finding a trail—the wide trail he had followed up the ridge yesterday. Would there be anything left of it?

He found it, just an indentation in the snow, after he left the last clearing. Now the going was faster, although his legs gave out every once in a while, sending him to his knees in the snow. He began to think about a warm cabin. Some hot cocoa. Those caribou steaks.

The trail ended at the lake, and he dragged himself out onto the ice. He paused to rest. His cabin, on the other side of the lake, looked like a black dot in the snow. Could he make it that far?

A round figure bundled in furs came hurrying toward him. Nanouk.

"Steve! Where have you been? We look for you."

He tried to answer, but his lips were dry and cracked. Finally he got some words out. "Went up on the ridge. Got caught by that blizzard."

The Eskimo's strong arm was supporting him. "Oh, yes. We should have tell you. In this month, storms come fast. Your dog keep you okay?"

"Yes, okay."

"We look for you," Nanouk repeated. "Today we talk about that book of Mark you bring."

"What?"

"Today is time for meetings," said Nanouk. "After kill bear, mens can do no work for three days."

Steve smiled, tasting blood as his lips cracked and split. *Thank you, Lord.*

He smiled again. "Sounds good to me."

14 He Going to Die

"It was amazing," Steve said. He tightened his seat belt as the little Cub bounced through a patch of turbulence. "I mean, I had given up on this trip. And God had it all planned—the bear and everything."

Jackson sent the plane up through an opening between two clouds. His voice came clearly through the headset and it sounded like he was grinning. "You were amazed? I thought you were so sure God had some reason for you to stay there while I went off and had fun."

"Yeah." Here above the clouds, the sun shone brilliantly, lighting up the tops of the clouds as if they were made of fresh snow. Every once in a while, Steve caught a glimpse of white mountain ridges sliding past below them.

That night in the storm had been rough, but he'd lived through it okay, and something important had happened to him. For once he hadn't panicked. God had enabled him to hang on to His promise and had given him new confidence.

"You know, all I was hoping for was to preach a couple of times. But the Lord arranged for two whole days of meetings while they couldn't work, and the Nanouks invited me for supper *and* Bible study both nights. Then today, the men could have started building their store again, but we had a wonderful long meeting that lasted until you flew in this afternoon."

"So they liked the Gospels of Mark?"

"Sure did. At Bible study, Nanouk read a section in Eskimo, then we sat around and talked about what God was saying. I gave away every single copy. Nanouk's going to keep up with the Bible study."

The clouds had begun to disperse, and the white tundra flats stretched out below them. No sign of caribou. Or wolves.

Inevitably, the thought of wolves reminded him of the Danner woman. What was she up to these days? How was Liz? And Charlie? He could hardly wait to get back to Koyalik.

Soon now. They had passed over Shanaluk, and Jackson was flying down the Tiskleet River, gradually descending. There was the airstrip.

Jackson made a low pass to check it out, as he always did. It looked fine.

The skis kicked up a flurry of loose snow as the Cub touched down, and they slid to a stop near the end of the airstrip. Mikki whined expectantly, and Steve leaned over the seat to free him from the net. He scratched behind the floppy ear. "It's good to get back, isn't it, boy?"

He climbed stiffly out of the plane, and Liz was there, waiting for him.

Something had happened.

As soon as he saw her face, he could tell that it was something bad, but she didn't say anything as they unloaded the airplane, said *thank-you* and *goodbye* to Jackson and waved him off.

She knelt to give Mikki a proper welcoming hug, speaking in the special crooning voice she kept for him. When she finally stood up, she was blinking back tears. Steve put an arm around her and all he could think to say was, "You okay?"

She nodded, then said in a choked voice, "The dogs . . ."

"What happened to them?"

"Patch died this morning."

"*Patch?* How come?"

Liz shook her head and picked up his duffle bag. "Nobody knows why. Two village dogs died yesterday and three more today."

She started down the icy path as if she were in a hurry to get to the cabin.

Steve, suddenly aware that Mikki had bounded almost out of sight, called him back. "Mikki, here!" He picked up the rest of his gear and followed Liz, with Mikki prancing beside them.

The three remaining dogs greeted him with howls of welcome. "Hey there, Bigfoot!" called Steve. "Hey, Bandit! Hey, Howler!" He fed Mikki and chained him in his usual place. No matter what, it was good to be back.

He glanced at Tignak's cabin. It was quiet over there. Tignak's dogs were gone. He went inside with a hundred questions for Liz.

She put his duffle bag on the bunk but didn't move to unpack it. "Gus took a close look at those dead dogs this morning," she said. "At first he thought they'd caught distemper or something, but they live in different parts of the village. He said one of them looked like it had been drooling."

"Like it ate something." Steve leaned against the table, thinking aloud. "Ate something bad. But these dogs can eat just about anything. Had to be something really bad."

Liz waited, her eyes wide and anxious.

"So what's Gus think? Poison?"

She nodded.

He took a deep breath and stood up to pace back and forth in the little cabin. The caribou antlers by the stove caught his eye, reminding him of all that God had promised.

He stopped pacing. "Where'd Tignak go?"

"To Tagatok, on Wednesday. His sister was very sick."

"Did Charlie go with him?"

"No. He's been around, but come to think of it, I haven't seen him all day."

"I'm going over there."

"I'm going with you."

The grandmother let them in with smiles and exclamations of welcome. Sarah came out from a back room. She ran to Liz and clung to her hand.

"What's the matter, Sarah?" asked Liz. "Where's Charlie?"

"Nothing matter. But I worry. Charlie come in a big rush. Had to take white woman somewhere right away. When she tell him something, he always have to hurry."

"But your father has the dog team, right?" asked Liz.

"Yes. Charlie borrow dogs from Victor."

"Where did your brother go?" asked Steve.

"Up the river. He say he come back tonight, not worry."

Dread clamped down upon Steve, and he shook it off. "Well," he said, "then we won't worry. But the minute that young scalawag gets home, tell him to come see me."

Sarah nodded. "I tell him. Scalawag." He knew she would add that word to her collection of strange American expressions.

Silently they walked back to their own cabin in the fading afternoon light. The four dogs made welcoming noises, as if they'd been away all day.

Steve spoke to them affectionately. Good dogs. But Patch was gone. One of the best. How was he going to manage with only four dogs?

Lord, protect our dogs, he prayed.

Over supper he told Liz about the bear and the storm and the way God had arranged for the meetings. She brightened, and he knew that the good news had encouraged her.

While they talked, he kept an eye on Tignak's cabin. Lights came on, but all was still quiet. Then there was a commotion of dogs. Charlie must have come back.

Steve waited, expecting to hear the boy's voice at the door. He picked up a harness and checked it for worn spots. Yes, one place to mend . . . Poison? Where was he going to get another dog? Good dogs were expensive . . . *Poison?*

"Does Gus have any ideas about this poison?" he asked.

"Well, he said some people up around Nome are using poison on the wolves, but no one in Koyalik would have anything to do with that."

The boy certainly was taking his time getting over here. Maybe Sarah had forgotten to tell him. No, Sarah wouldn't forget. Maybe he had more important things to do.

Steve put away his gear, cleaned his rifle, and helped to dry the dishes.

"Well, I'm not going to wait around all night for Charlie," he said finally. He put on his parka. "I think I'll go up to the Trading Post and ask Gus."

The dogs yipped and snarled beside the cabin. A woman cried out.

Then came Charlie's voice. "Steve!"

He rushed outside.

Charlie was kneeling beside Mikki. Beyond him in the deep snow, Elsa Danner struggled to sit up.

"Steve." Charlie's voice shook. "She—she give something to Mikki. He going to die."

Steve dropped to his knees beside the dog. "What'd she do?"

"She throw something to Mikki. And Bandit. They eat it fast before I can get it."

"Okay, now listen," said Steve. "Go help Liz. I need lots of salt and a cup. And a pot of water and something to stir with—quick!"

He put a hand on Mikki's shoulder. The dog lifted his head and growled at Elsa Danner.

The woman pulled herself to her feet. She stepped onto the path, brushing snow from her clothes.

"That boy knocked me over," she said in a low, deadly voice. "And he incited that wolf of yours to attack me."

Steve glanced past her. Sarah and a couple of Eskimo men had arrived. "Henry," he said, "keep the white woman here. Do not let her go anywhere."

Henry moved to Elsa Danner's side.

"Sarah—go find Gus," he said. "Hurry."

Charlie came running out of the cabin with Liz close behind.

Steve took the pot from him. "Okay. Mikki first. You two hold him. He won't like this." Quickly Steve dipped out a cup of water, poured salt into it, and stirred. He held the dog's muzzle in one hand, covering the nose to make him open his mouth. Then he poured in the salt mixture and held the muzzle shut while Mikki swallowed convulsively.

"Sorry, boy."

Mikki's eyes opened wide, but he did not resist.

"Now some water. You've got to have water." He poured two cupfuls of water down the dog's throat. "Maybe that'll do it."

His hands were wet and getting colder by the minute. He wiped them on his parka. "Let's do Bandit."

As he knelt over the dog, Elsa Danner began to complain about the cold, but she stopped in mid-sentence. Good for you, Henry, he thought.

Bandit struggled and backed away, growling, but one of the men helped Charlie hold him still and they finally got the salt solution and water down him.

Liz had just brought out more salt and water when Gus came striding through the snow. He was still pulling on his mittens. "What's going on?"

Before Steve could answer, Mikki lurched to his feet and began to vomit. "Good dog!" exclaimed Steve. "Good boy! Get rid of it!"

He knelt to examine the snow. "Here." From the remains of Mikki's supper he picked up what looked like a round chunk of light-colored meat. "Charlie, how many pieces did she give them?"

"Just one, I think." Charlie made a small, strangled sound. "She throw food to three other dogs tonight," he said.

Gus seemed to understand what was going on. "What're you using for an emetic? Salt? Good. Charlie, show us which dogs."

Gus and four Eskimo men took the salt and water and disappeared into the darkness with Charlie.

"Steve?" Liz's face was pale. "Mrs. Danner is cold. May she come inside?"

"Okay, but Henry, stay with her. Liz, could you bring me some more water?"

They went into the cabin, but Steve could not leave Mikki. He held the dog's face close to his own and scratched behind the floppy ear. Maybe it was a slow-dissolving poison.

He glanced at Bandit. "Come on, boy, get rid of it."

Liz brought out another pot of water and waited with him, her hand on Mikki's head. Finally Bandit stood up, making sounds of distress, and vomited. Steve picked out a piece of meat that matched the other. Then he gave more water to both dogs.

His hands were numb and his feet were stinging with cold. He'd better go inside. They could take Mikki with them and keep an eye on him. Bandit wasn't used to being in the cabin; he'd be okay outside.

Flashlights and a crunching in the snow told him that Gus was returning. Charlie came too, but not the Eskimo men. They were probably taking care of the dogs.

Together they went into the cabin. Gus pulled off his stocking cap, and gray hair stood up in wisps around his bald spot. "Your dogs okay? Maybe we got to the others in time."

They took off their parkas, and the trader muttered, "Where's that stuff she gave your dogs?" He held out a big hand, and Steve put one of the meat chunks into it.

Gus sat down and held it under the lantern on the table. "Bacon?" He glanced up at Steve. "Like candy to a dog. But not many Eskimos buy bacon."

Gus pulled out his knife. The bacon had been sewn around a piece of seal blubber, and he slit it open. Inside was a small white tablet, partially dissolved.

Gus muttered something, staring at it. His forehead turned red.

Elsa Danner was sitting beside the stove, drinking tea. She leaned back when Gus held the meat in front of her nose.

"Where did you get this?" he thundered. "What kind of poison is it, woman?"

"I beg your pardon?" She lifted her chin. "Steve, what's the matter with this man?"

Steve ignored her. "Liz, please get us some coffee. Charlie, you want tea? Henry? Gus, please sit down."

Liz filled their mugs in silence. Elsa Danner sipped at her tea, looking offended. Charlie accepted a mug from Liz but did not sit down. He leaned against the wall, clutching it in both hands.

Finally Steve spoke. "Gus, I think we need to hear what Charlie has to say."

The boy's hands tightened on the mug until his knuckles turned white. "I should know better. She have bad spirit in her, tungak. I feel it today."

"Start at the beginning," said Gus.

"Mrs. Danner, lotsa time, she tell me to do things help her. One day she want seal so she can use teeth and claws. I get for her. One day she want lotsa ptarmigan. I shoot them. Every night she walk down to ice and stand there. I curious, and I follow. I track her like I track fox. So she not know. She talk to the seals."

"Nonsense!" exclaimed Elsa Danner.

Henry nodded. "I see her do this every night." His dark face held a glimmer of amusement. "I see Charlie too, but she do not."

Elsa Danner frowned at Charlie, but he went on.

"One day she tell me to take her up river so she can look at animal tracks and walk on tundra. We find tracks by river bank, and she tell me, 'Stay with dogs.' Then she say, 'I want to talk to spirit of wolves.' She carry bag with her."

"What day was this?" asked Gus.

"The day Steve go away in Sugar Dog."

"Tuesday," Liz said.

Charlie nodded. "That night she walk down to ice again. After she talk to seals, she stop and talk to dogs on way back to cabin. Then next night same thing. But I see her throw something to dogs, and they eat it."

"Wednesday, right?" said Gus.

"Yes."

Elsa Danner put down her mug, and tea spilled over the edge. "This is ridiculous. He can't prove any of it. The kid's got a grudge against me all of a sudden. Maybe I didn't pay him enough. Who knows?"

Her face changed as she looked at Charlie. "What's the matter, boy?" Steve had never heard her use such a soft, wheedling tone. "We used to be good friends. You told me all about your family and how you want to go to the States and how you're saving up for that knife. Don't tell lies about me. I haven't forgotten about those seal claws you want. I can help you."

Charlie's eyes were black slits in his face. He looked at Steve. "At first she very nice. Then she tell me you doing bad things. She say you come to make Eskimos poor so you get rich. I know this is lies. I want the knife, so I say nothing. But I start to watch her."

"There, you see, he admits it," exclaimed Elsa Danner. "The kid goes around spying on people. And who knows what else he's been doing? One of my rings is missing, by the way. He needs to be locked up."

She stood to her feet, and Mikki sat up, eyeing her.

She held out a hand to Gus. "I appeal to you as the only sane white person in this village. I lodge a formal complaint against this boy. He knocked me to the ground—that's a case of assault and battery. He has not even apologized for such behavior, and furthermore—"

"Mrs. Danner, please sit down," said Gus. His voice was low, but his forehead had flushed angrily again. "Go on, Charlie."

The boy glanced at Steve, who nodded encouragement. "Today she tell me take her up the river like before. She carry bag with her, same way. We stop in willows and she tell me to stay with dogs, but this time I watch her. She walk out on tundra and drop the ptarmigan I shoot for her, one here, one there."

"He couldn't see that from the willows," interrupted Elsa Danner.

"Yes, he could," Gus said impatiently. "Eskimos have excellent eyesight. Go on, Charlie."

"After she come back, I start thinking about who would eat the birds. May be wolves."

"And what's so terrible about that?" Elsa Danner's voice rose. "The government of Alaska pays a bounty on wolves and permits the use of poison. I haven't done anything wrong."

She glared at them. "I hate those evil creatures. They murder my caribou. I talked to the men in the village about having a wolf hunt, and all they could tell me was some nonsense about wolf spirits. And this village is full of wolves, so I took matters into my own hands." She shrugged daintily. "I don't see what all the fuss is about."

Charlie went on as if she had not spoken. "And I think about how the dogs in the village get sick and die. She hate Mikki because he look like wolf, I know that. So I watch when she take her walk tonight by Steve's cabin. She throw something to Mikki and to Bandit. Then I give her a little push."

"A little push! He knocked me right over."

"Enough." Gus stood to his feet. "What kind of poison? Where did you get it?"

"That's really no business of yours. But I got it quite legally from a friend of mine in the States, and you should know that it's not against the law to use Compound 1080 on wolves."

Gus glanced at Steve, looking relieved. "Compound 1080. Odorless, tasteless. But it takes four to ten hours to work." He reached for his parka. "Come on, Mrs. Danner, let's go."

"Go where? I'm going right back to my cabin, and you cannot stop me."

"If you value your life, I'd suggest that you sleep at the Trading Post tonight, ma'am. Pack your things and leave Koyalik on Monday when the mail plane comes in. Eskimos have a very simple system of justice."

She made an indignant sound and he held up one hand. "You have killed several good dogs—their means of transportation, their means of getting food, one of the most valuable commodities in this wild country."

"But the law—"

"I refuse to answer for your safety." The old trader stared at her with cold blue eyes. "No doubt you have deeply offended these people. And you yourself have remarked that they are superstitious. Who knows what they may decide to do to you?"

15 Funny-looking

"I'm glad nothing happened to her," said Liz. "But I sure felt like singing when that plane took off this afternoon." She began stacking up the supper plates.

"Me too." Steve still had a mouthful of pie.

"Do you think she'll come back?"

"No." Tignak looked up from cutting his pie into neat squares. "Gus said she made some rather pointed comments about the hostility of the natives in this village. She's going to do the rest of her research in Nome and Kotzebue."

Liz refilled their mugs with tea and sat down again. "I've been watching Mikki pretty closely, all day yesterday and today. He seems fine, doesn't he?"

"Yes, and Bandit's already gotten into another fight," said Steve.

"I'll miss Patch." Liz looked down into her mug. "That woman did a lot of harm. I'm still worried about Charlie."

"Don't stop praying for him," said Tignak.

"We won't," said Steve. Unfortunately, Charlie would remember Elsa Danner for a long time. She'd been a bad influence on Victor and Nida too. But he wasn't going to give up on them either.

He glanced at the stack of red Bibles on their bookshelf. Still four of them left.

"Tignak, do you think the people really would have . . . done something to her?" asked Liz.

He shook his head. "Not here. Koyalik is a somewhat modern village, right here on the coast. But inland . . ."

"Oh!" exclaimed Steve. "I didn't get a chance to tell you about the bear at Mierow Lake." He described what had happened when he and Jackson had killed the bear.

Tignak listened, nodding. "The Eskimo lives in fear," he said. "He is aware of being very small and powerless in a world that is huge and terrifying and full of mysteries he can't understand. That fear is the reason for taboos and amulets and such things. I can say that because I felt afraid too, even though I thought of myself as a modern Eskimo. The old ways and the old fears are very strong. But Jesus Christ is stronger, and now that I belong to Him, He has set me free."

He ate the last crumbs of pie crust on his plate. "You know, at Tagatok this time, a few people actually listened to me. I told them I was not afraid any more because of this Person who had changed my life. My sister died, but I think she knew Christ, at the end. She was not afraid, and they noticed that."

Liz glanced at Steve. "If only Tignak could talk to that bunch at Mierow Lake."

"Yes," Tignak said, as if he'd read her thoughts. "You could borrow a dog, and maybe we could make one more trip before—"

"Before what?"

Tignak smiled at her. "It's almost May. Snow melts, you know."

"Oh, that's right!" Liz picked up a pile of dishes and took them to the sink. "How else could we get there, anyway? The Cub is too small for all of us."

"Well, it's a long walk," said Steve. He'd been thinking about how hard it would be to get around without a dog sled. There weren't any roads. "Maybe we could take canoes from one river to the next. That's what they did in the good ol' days. Or buy a boat with an outboard motor. But I'm not sure if we'd end up at Mierow Lake."

"Doesn't sound very promising," said Liz. She poured hot water over the dishes. "So, shall we try to get back there right away . . . maybe next week? I'll come and do stories with the children. Oh! Who's that?"

She turned to the door. "C'mon in, Charlie."

"Hello, *whatzcookin?* Smells good in here." Charlie grinned and dropped a handful of letters onto the table. "Gus late sorting mail so he tell me bring yours."

One letter slid across the table on its own. Steve could tell by the long gray envelope that it was from the Mission. He did not move to pick it up.

Charlie stepped closer and eyed the half-empty pie plate. "I'll get you some pie," said Liz. "It's the blueberry-walnut kind you like."

Tignak followed the direction of Steve's gaze. "Don't want to open it?"

"Well, I'm sure wondering," said Steve. "I haven't had much good news to tell them lately. Come to think of it, I forgot to send in the last report. I hope they haven't decided that we're wasting our time."

But even as he spoke, he was surprised at the calm he felt. He continued his banter with Tignak. "Let's face it. I'm a coward."

Tignak cocked his head. "Perhaps Liz is brave enough to read the letter?"

Steve grinned. "She takes these things better than I do. She's got nerves of steel."

"All right, then!" Liz dried her hands on a towel, flipped it onto the caribou antlers, and came to stand beside Steve. She picked up the letter, opening it with a flourish.

"Dear Steve and Liz,"

Her voice changed. "They want us to come back—come back to the States—because—Steve—because—" She grabbed for his arm. "Because there's an airplane! Peter's church—Steve, *there's an airplane.* And we have to go pick it up . . ."

Tignak grinned. "Better read the letter, coward."

Quickly Steve scanned the letter, which told how Peter's church had joined with their other supporting churches to buy an airplane for the Koyalik work.

He started to speak, then had to look down at the letter again to see if he'd read it right. Yes, a plane.

He cleared his throat. "We're supposed to go down to San Francisco early this summer to look at it."

Tignak's face glowed. "What kind?"

"A Cessna 170. Needs some work, but it's got low engine time. After we fix it up, we'll fly it back to Koyalik in the fall."

Charlie looked up from his pie. "How big? Like the Cub?"

"Bigger. Carries four people and baggage. Faster too."

Liz looked around the table, and her smile dimmed. "I wish we didn't have to be away all summer."

Tignak shrugged. "Most people leave the village in summer. They go to squirrel camp and then fish camp and so on. Mosquitoes here grow as big as rabbits. Summer is the best time to be away."

Charlie peered at the letter. "Your airplane—do it have name like that Sugar Dog?"

"Yes, let's see," said Steve. "Its number is 1577 Zebra."

Charlie looked puzzled. "A zebra? Oh, I know. Caribou with black and white stripes." He grinned. "Funny-looking airplane."

Liz gave him a friendly nudge. "Very funny, Charlie. You just wait and see. When we come flying back here next fall, you will be amazed at our wonderful and *not* funny-looking airplane!"

Charlie sobered, as if he had just realized that they would be gone for three months.

He gave Steve a solemn look, then his eyes brightened with anticipation. "I wait for you to come back. And I will be amazed."